THE HEART'S JOURNEY HOME

THE HEART'S JOURNEY HOME

A Quest for Wisdom

NICHOLAS HARNAN, M.S.C.

AVE MARIA PRESS
Notre Dame, Indiana 46556

To my father and mother, who travelled their road heroically and wisely and allowed their story to unfold lovingly.

To my brothers, John and Jim, and my sister, Sheila, and their families, who made the back roads of life so enriching and affirming.

Excerpts from *The Little Prince* by Antoine de Saint Exupéry, copyright © 1943 and renewed 1971 by Harcourt Brace Jovanovich, Inc., reprinted by permission of the publisher.

Excerpts from THE JERUSALEM BIBLE, copyright © 1966 by Darton, Longman & Todd, Ltd. and Doubleday & Company, Inc. Used by permission of the publisher.

International Standard Book Number: 0-87793-478-9
                                     0-87793-477-0 (pbk.)

Library of Congress Catalog Card Number: 91-77475

Cover and text design by Elizabeth J. French

Printed and bound in the United States of America.

Contents

Introduction

We live in an age of transition in which an old order is breaking down and a new one is beginning to emerge. This has been extensively chronicled by many writers and prophets of recent times.[1] This book addresses just one of the many aspects of this transition. Any authentic change in global consciousness and paradigm awareness must surely be rooted in the heart of the individual and involve personal transformation. The new order must be securely established in our hearts if we are to be people of a new age and a new global vision. While this book might appear to concentrate on personal growth and development to the exclusion of communal concerns and obligations, in reality, the two are inextricably bound. Only when we undertake the journey to the heart can we begin to resonate with the hearts of others and with the heart of God. In other words, once we begin to find our real selves, we also find other people at a level of love close to that exercised by Christ as he walked among us. We discover that God longs for the fulfillment of his dream for his creation. This book attempts to elucidate that profound challenge presented to the human family by Christ when he said: "You must love your neighbor as yourself."

Numerous books have already been written on this subject and it could be claimed that anything worth saying on the matter has already been said. Because of this belief I resisted writing this book for many years. The persistence of friends and participants in my conferences and workshops finally persuaded me to put pen to paper or, more precisely, finger to word processor! A central theme in their attempts to persuade me might be articulated in the following manner — *since authentic human growth is an integral part of Christian spirituality but, unfortunately, was sometimes ignored in the past, any attempt to reinforce this truth is never superfluous.*[2]

One last word of caution: If you are a sophisticated traveler to the heart, having studied many of the great maps already available, and are anxious to glean quickly every possible item of information to enhance your sophistication, do not bother with this book.

But if you are still lost, or confused by all the modern expertise now available, then it might be worth your while to continue. Some of us are old-fashioned travelers. We have not yet learned how to find our way on modern highways. So we are forced to travel on foot through the back roads and country lanes. This way is slow, inefficient, and laborious. But it has one distinct advantage. You could meet some very interesting characters who will enrich your journey. In fact some people claim to have met Christ as they laboriously headed for another Emmaus in an attempt to escape the mystery of their story. Because they eschewed modern transport and decided to walk, they fortuitously fell into step with a stranger who gave them the real directions for their journey. My wish is that once you embark upon this old-fashioned journey, willing to walk the way of the heart, you too may meet a stranger, fall in step, and end up hearing the story burning to be told in the depths of your heart.

NICHOLAS HARNAN, M.S.C.
May 30, 1990

Part 1

In Search of a Road...

1

Life Is a Journey

Once upon a time a distraught tourist was trying to negotiate a maze of back roads in a remote corner of Ireland. After a lengthy search for her friend's house she concluded that she was hopelessly lost. Coming upon an old gentleman sitting at the side of the road, she stopped her automobile and, with some embarrassment, told the old man that she could not find her way to her friend's house. He reassured her kindly. "Dear lady, you are not as lost as you might think. You managed to find me, didn't you? And sure I know the way to your friend's house. So let us see how best I can direct you."

Through this book, let us go on a journey together, a very old journey that has been made since the beginning of time, the journey of life assigned to all of us by God at the moment of our creation. It is an interior journey, a journey to the heart of our lives. It challenges us to grow into the people God has called us to be. Since it is a very old journey, on a road that has been traveled by many people down through the centuries, long before the discoveries of our modern technological age, it might be wise to stay with an old way of describing it. The old way relies heavily on imagery and story rather than on ideas and logical propositions. It is a well-tried method in the history of education and was effectively employed by the greatest teacher of all time, Jesus.

This age-old journey may have become more complicated for us today because we have lost touch with the old ways of wisdom and tradition. These were long in the making and are couched in a language and an approach more in tune with the heart of the human family than with modern studies in psychology. We will reflect on this as we go.

When God called us into life, he called us to embark upon a very special journey. This journey began at the moment of our conception, and continues until the moment of our death. It is a journey with a sacred purpose, exquisitely designed to foster our full human growth and spiritual development. It is destined to be an unfolding of that beautiful plan implanted by God in our hearts at the moment of our creation, the realization of God's dream for us. This journey has to do with growth toward maturity at every level — physical, intellectual, moral, emotional, and spiritual. The process of becoming the persons God intends us to be has been graced by the coming of Jesus into our world. By taking on our full human experience and the challenge of a human life, he has accomplished the human journey. He now walks with us every step of the way and offers us an experience of growth full of faith, hope, and love.

But in spite of the presence of Jesus with us, our journey in life can be misdirected, misunderstood, and even abandoned. Much unhappiness in the world today is caused by the painful experience of being lost spiritually. For many people the road of life that stretches out in front of them might appear meaningless and cruel. The rising and the falling, the twists and the turns might be interpreted as just so many additional irritants on a tiresome journey undertaken with little conviction and even less enthusiasm. The temptation must surely be great to try to avoid the journey by getting involved in activities that distract them from the pressing invitation of Jesus to follow him.

Let us return to our opening story and see what more we can learn about the nature of journeying. Our tourist friend has learned a very vivid lesson about roads: there are two types of roads — main roads that are clearly posted, and numerous back roads that are often infuriatingly anonymous. These back roads call for a completely different system of direction-finding. Our tourist, accustomed to modern travel on sophisticated highways, finds such skills beyond her competence. She must turn to a local inhabitant, such as the old gentleman sitting by the roadside. He knows these back roads by heart, not by signposts. He relates to these back roads differently than a tourist. This difference in attitude is very simply explained. The local inhabitant is at *home* here. The tourist is on a visit, and is happy to remain a stranger, provided she has easy access to the reassurance of the main thoroughfare.

In much the same way, our journey in life has its own special pattern, made up of main roads of everyday living and those smaller back roads that draw us toward the heart of our life. This pattern, expertly designed by God, brings out our deeper, hidden, but real self, which is the goal of our journey of growth.

Unfortunately, for some of us, the wide, direct main roads of life take up all our attention and interest. Restricting our journey to these roads reinforces the presence of our false self. We may even consider the back roads, with their twists and turns leading us into uncharted areas, to be unhealthy and dangerous. Many of us avoid them at all costs.

If our unique journey in life, however, is to teach us how to be real people, then we must follow all the roads laid down for us by God — especially our back roads.

While many of these roads are still shrouded in mystery and fear, they nevertheless are the only access to the core of who we really are. If we stay too long with the speed and security of the principal highways, we could miss the people, the houses, the memories, the experiences waiting to identify us on the back roads. If we are diverted by accident on to one of these back roads, we tend to ignore the rich countryside through which this tiny road wends its way because of our hectic rush to regain the main road. We may even curse the bother of being trapped in what we consider to be hostile countryside.

Is it any wonder that at times we feel unreal, alienated from our true center, and unsure of the direction that will produce real happiness and peace? Sadly, we often seek our peace and reassurance in another frantic trip down the highway of our false self. Only when we have succeeded in sorting out the difference in roads, and know something of what we can expect to find at the end of them, will we be ready for a clearer understanding of the difference between the real and the false self.

To be fair, some people do occasionally venture down the back roads of their lives very much by design. In fact they often pride themselves on their resourcefulness and on the spirit of adventure involved in these trips into self-analysis. In a genuine quest for deeper self-knowledge or relief from some emotional bondage, these courageous people are prepared to spend considerable amounts of money and time in the exploration of the back roads of their personal history. The results of these psychotherapeutic, self-reflective, or counseling exercises are often rich and rewarding. However, we might ask about the spiritual quality of these self-exploratory excursions: What is the quality of their *relationship* to these sacred back roads?

There are three possible relationships to the back roads of our lives. First, there is the relationship of avoidance. This person avoids growth by ignoring the back roads. The journey becomes distorted because all attention and energy are devoted to developing greater speed and efficiency on the main roads. If by accident one of the abandoned back roads is encountered, every effort is made to scramble back to the main road as quickly as possible.

Second, there is the relationship of the tourist, who is curious about what might be found farther away from the main road. An excursion is made in the hope of discovering some new sights or of generating some kind of meaningful experience. But when the adventure is over, and the tourist carries off these new discoveries as coveted trophies, he or she can still remain a stranger to the remote byways themselves. The reason for this might be found in the motivation for the excursion. Such people may lack a deep spiritual motivation, undertaking the exploration just to relieve emotional distress, believing that the source of their emotional struggles is to be found on one of the back roads of early life. Or the exploration of the back roads may have been undertaken in the desire for greater personal power or fulfillment. The end result in such cases is an attitude of estrangement. The back roads are not accepted as being special channels of God's presence in one's life. They are simply used to attain a certain level of experience and are quickly forgotten once the security of the main road has been regained.

Third, there is the relationship of the local inhabitant, who regards these back roads as an integral part of his or her own world. Such people truly live there and allow these mysterious back roads to lead them to their home. Feeling comfortable themselves in traveling these back roads, they are always willing to spend some time helping a lost tourist to shed the attitude of stranger and become one of their own. Most of us would like to travel this way — if we dared.

We consider all roads of life, be they main roads or back roads, to be of deep spiritual significance. What matters is the unique pattern of these two kinds of roads. Part of our journey will be made on the open and fast highways, part will be made on the back roads. These back roads are the early roads of our childhood, and we must revisit them as adults in order to recover and fulfill the whole plan of our development as envisioned by God. We must learn to feel at home and to know these roads by heart. These roads give real direction and will lead us to our ultimate home in the heart of the blessed trinity.

At the end of one of our obscure back roads we may find our real home, our true center, the heart of our lives. Jesus wishes to accompany us to this deep interior center. He has given us the assurance that the home we will find there is God's house, a mansion in which there are many rooms. Because of our sinful loss of trust in God, we may have abandoned this sacred house and gone in search of a house of our own making. This is the original sin. Jesus came to save us from this foolish and reckless journey. He has become for us the way, the truth, and the life. Everything he taught us while on earth was designed to teach us how to make this journey, a journey to the heart of the trinity dwelling in the depths of our being. On the night before he died he left us final instructions. In John's gospel we read:

> "Do not let your hearts be troubled.
> Trust in God still, and trust in me.
> There are many rooms in my Father's house;
> if there were not, I should have told you.

I am going now to prepare a place for you,
    and after I have gone and prepared you a place,
I shall return to take you with me;
so that where I am
you may be too.
You know the way to the place
    where I am going" (Jn 14:1–4).

This very moving assurance from Jesus reminds me of a story about a young boy who lived with his parents and baby sister in a nice house. He began to behave in a strange manner, especially as nightfall approached. Many times he was found running away as if to escape from something frightening within the house. At last the explanation was uncovered. Since the family was not using all the space in the house, one room upstairs was left unfurnished and locked up. At night the boy frequently explored the house and became very curious about the locked room. One night he listened outside the door of this locked room and, to his horror, he heard a dragon hissing inside. The house took on a terrifying atmosphere because of the danger it harbored in this room.

To help reconcile the boy with the house and dispel this fearful threat, an exercise to expel this dragon was mounted. The father brought the boy to the bottom of the stairs and explained what he was going to do. The boy would stay with his mother while he, the father, would go on ahead, unlock the door, search the room, and make sure it was quite safe. Then he would come back and take the boy with him into the room. They explored the room together, but found no sign of a dragon. Then the father noticed a paper bag on the floor. He saw unmistakable signs that mice had been in this bag quite often. The father explained to the boy that in the stillness of an empty room a mouse rummaging in a paper bag could create a sound like a dragon hissing. The boy's fears were dispelled because he made a journey in the safe company of his father to discover the source of his crippling fears. Because of this healing journey the boy was able to move freely about his house and feel at home once more.

This story comes to mind when I encounter someone who is afraid to make an interior journey of healing and liberation. Many people fail to make this journey and allow their mansion, with its many rooms, to remain locked up and abandoned. They imagine these empty, unexplored rooms to be inhabited by ghosts and dragons. A convenient room near the front of the house is occupied and all manner of hectic activity is concentrated there, lending a pathetic dignity to the neglected house. At times this front room is turned into a prayer room in a misguided attempt to confine God to this limited space. Meanwhile God comes to the door in various disguises, asking to be let into the warmth and comfort of our other rooms. Many times this stranger is turned away unwelcomed and unblessed because of our fears of the locked rooms and the demons we think are hiding there. Jesus has come into our lives with the good news. He has gone on ahead of us, checked out our rooms, expelled the demons. He now comes back for us to take us with him on this interior journey of growth and liberation. He wants us to be where he is now, in the heart of our life.

Our journey of growth and healing is necessary because it frees God in our hearts and in our interior home. It opens up the fullness of our personhood, allowing God to walk freely in his own house and to receive the stranger who may need temporary shelter for the night or comfort from the warm hospitality of our inner parlors. It allows God to be God in the home he originally designed and now anxiously wants to restore.

I remember vividly an old house being restored when I was a child. For years it lay abandoned and neglected, filled with ghosts and creatures from the wilds. One front room was occasionally used as a workshop and the debris of broken machinery spilled out onto the unkept lawn. Then new owners took over the house and restoration began. Every day as we came home from school we saw new and exciting improvements. The briars and the rubbish were cleared from the path leading to the front door. Inside the house each room was cleared, cleaned, repaired, and repainted. The day the front door was opened was the day that smoke first appeared from the chimney. It was as exciting as raising someone from the dead. Each day the house took on more and more life. One day we were allowed inside. The house had been transformed. The ghosts and other unwelcome creatures had been expelled. It was now a home, offering warmth and hospitality. But most important of all it now spread this warmth to the whole neighborhood and to all who passed near this house.

This is the transformation that can take place if we embark upon our journey to the heart. Let us not be like some unfortunate people who eke out a dreary existence in one room and try to endure the threats of unknown dangers behind the doors of their many locked rooms. The lack of joy and growth in their beautiful mansion must cause serious concern to the Lord. It was to such neglected people that Jesus addressed his heartfelt cry of longing and compassion. "And when he saw the crowds he felt sorry for them because they were harassed and dejected, like sheep without a shepherd. Then he said to his disciples, 'The harvest is rich but the laborers are few, so ask the Lord of the harvest to send laborers to his harvest' " (Mt 9:36–37). The harvest could be likened to the undeveloped riches lying uncelebrated in the hearts of God's precious creation. The laborers are those special people God sends into our lives and along our journey to help us find the way to our hearts and to the many abandoned rooms there.

God provides us with all that is necessary for us to complete our sacred journey. Many of us need a guide to help us make our way through the more confusing back roads of our life. Having arrived at our unrestored house, we may also need a trusted companion to walk gently with us as we fearfully explore our house and open locked rooms. This trusted companion can also help us to see and clear away the briars and the debris that obscure the true beauty of our house. These special people may be near us or waiting for us further down our road. Sadly, many of them go unrecognized because we stay with the security of our main roads or travel so fast that we do not have time to greet them. Some of these special people may be spiritual directors, counselors, or psychotherapists. Many hold no such official position. They may be a good friend, a religious colleague, a casual acquaintance, the writer of a book, the preacher of a sermon — any of the many ingenious channels through which God speaks to us outside of a formal context of prayer. One thing we can be certain of — God is with us on our journey. He told us so. He has already gone on ahead of us and explored our house with its many rooms. He has prepared a special place for us to be with him there, in our hearts. There is nothing to be afraid of on our journey and in our house. The ghosts and dragons have been expelled. But much work of restoration needs to be done. We must not expect God to do it alone as if the laws of his creation did not exist. God will stay with the reality and process of our human growth. This is the channel through which he floods us with his grace. And in his speaking to us, we must not expect disembodied voices from the dark. God speaks to us through living people. Through them he shepherds us on our journey.

Before we conclude this chapter we need to remind each other that patience with our struggles is vitally necessary. We are limited, vulnerable, and fallible. We must be gentle with ourselves when we get lost or make a mistake, especially when we are in unknown territory. We must be compassionate to anyone struggling to make it to home.

Even people on the secure, wide, and clearly posted highways can have difficulty with their journeys. One particular character from my childhood had a special type of problem as he tried to make his way on foot along the main road. After a pint of beer too many, he found it a bit difficult to steady the road. A kind stranger met him one night and asked him, "Have you far to go?" My friend replied, "At this moment in time it is not the length of the road that bothers me. It is the width!"

Reflection Exercises

1. Spend a few minutes imagining your life so far in terms of a journey.

— Recall the principal stages of your journey in life so far.

— Can you identify any helpful strangers on your journey who helped you to find your way?

2. Begin today to keep a journal for your reflections

as you go through the exercises in this book. Also begin to draw up a comprehensive autobiography, beginning with a description of your parents and of your grandparents, if this is possible.

3. Thank God for the privilege of being invited on a unique journey to his home within us.

2

A Story for the Journey

Once upon a time there was a legendary character called the *Goban Saor*. He was a great builder of castles. One day he was asked to build a castle for a king in a foreign country, which would require a long journey to reach the place of work. Now the Goban had one son who was nearing adulthood. He decided to bring his son as company for the journey and also so that they might get to know one another better. They set out on their long journey. After a while the Goban said to his son, "Son, shorten the road for me." The son, thinking that the father meant the physical journey, pointed out some convenient short-cuts that avoided many of the twists and turns in the road. This approach did not please the Goban, so he said that they had better return home.

The next day they set out once more. After a while the Goban again said to his son, "Son, shorten the road for me." This time the son thought that the father wished to be distracted from the journey as a way of easing the burden of travel. So he tried to get his father deeply involved in a description of the castle he was going to build. The father was again disappointed and said that they had better return home.

That night the son confided his troubles to his mother. He told her about the mysterious test that he was being subjected to by his father. He desperately wanted to make this journey with his father and win his love and respect. The mother agreed to help him. She was a wise and compassionate woman and was anxious to make her son and her husband happy. So she told him the secret of shortening the road.

The next morning they set out on their journey once more. After some time the Goban asked his son to shorten the road for him. The son began to tell a story. In no time they had completed their journey. The father and the son established a strong bond of love between them because of the nature of their journey together.[3]

Our life can be compared to a journey; it can also be compared to a story unfolding on a journey. If we want to enter into the fullness of our story, then we must enter into the fullness of the journey. The main roads do not have the real history of our life. Some of the most important elements of our story must be traced down winding and narrow roads. But our journey is not always straightforward, as the story of the Goban and his son illustrates.

In his first attempt to shorten the journey the son offered a solution of which our modern technological world would approve. His suggestion of short-cuts was logical, efficient, and direct, the solution of road engineers who have laid down efficient highways as straight and as swift as the flight of an arrow. While our lives, to some degree, have been enriched by these modern developments, we need to remember that human beings are not the products of engineering resourcefulness. We are living people with a long history, and we must be loyal to the older and more mysterious pathways of life. This is true despite a growing attachment to speed, efficiency, and directness. This very attachment has created a crisis of identity in some people. They have allowed themselves to be defined by the main roads of their life and the value of their accomplishments. Their sense of self only feels real and authentic on the fast main roads. They overidentify with performance, roles, results, efficiency, and material success. But they end up as superficial shells.

In the son's second attempt to shorten the road he again resorted to a modern, familiar, and well tried tactic. He tried to distract the father by attempting to absorb him in highly functional matters. This is a common feature of many of our modern journeys. It is known as "killing the journey." Distractions are used as a kind of anesthetic against the experience of the journey. Distractions and pastimes can legitimately be used to give temporary relief from the burdens of life. But whenever these are used to escape from the central experience of the journey, then the story of the journey becomes impoverished and devalued.

Finally the Goban's son uncovered the real wisdom of the journey, a wisdom that might never have been uncovered had he not recognized two important things. First, he realized that he was stumped and did not know how to proceed. Second, he recognized in his mother a wise and understanding counselor who could offer him light for this part of his journey. Recognizing the need for a guide or a mentor at certain stages in our journey has been referred to already and will receive more attention in later chapters.

We may not immediately detect a difference between telling a story and the son's second tactic of distracting his father from the tedium of the journey. The difference lies in appreciating the original purpose of telling stories. Before our exposure to technology and the modern glorification of analytical thinking, the story was one of the principal means of communication. People were vitally connected to their past by means of stories passed on from one generation to another. Much of the education of both adults and children was conducted through the medium of story. Profound truths, especially of a spiritual nature, were illustrated and elaborated through story.

Story is a very old means of reaching the inner reality within each human person that we call the heart. Children are fascinated with stories. It may be that the child is hungry for reassurance and for familiar contact with a world that is welcoming and empowering. Story immediately opens up this kind of world and enables the child to feel connected with the sometimes baffling world of the adult.

While story was also used as a source of entertainment, it was never trivialized or distorted for other ends. Today we have lost some of our innocence in this area of entertainment. In the cinema, on television, and in cheap literature, story can be presented as mindless distraction and escape. From a superficial point of view it might appear that telling a story on a journey is essentially just another distracting tactic. On closer examination, however, we discover that in the distracting tactic we attempt to avoid full awareness of the journey, whereas through the story we can enter more deeply into the experience of the journey.

A spiritual journey is not a movement from one physical point to another. Rather, it is a deep interior movement from one level of spiritual and human growth to another. The quality of this journey is determined by the quality of the relationship we cultivate as we grow in knowledge of ourselves, of others, and of God. This intimate and self-revelatory knowledge is best communicated through the sensitive medium of story. Story can transcend the barriers that divide the human family.

One of the most important fruits of listening to God's story of our life is the development of authentic self-knowledge. God is with us on our journey. In his desire to reveal himself to us on the way, he reveals us to ourselves. He tells us the story of who we really are for him. Jesus continually offers us this kind of *self-knowledge* on every step of our journey. It is truly liberating, sacramental, and grace-filled. In and through such self-knowledge we learn not only about ourselves but also about God's redeeming action in our hearts. We call this self-knowledge "authentic" to distinguish it from the self-knowledge that is merely knowing *about* ourselves. Authentic self-knowledge is the story of who we are that is implanted by God at the beginning of our journey. To hear this authentic story we must, like the local inhabitant, be truly at home in the back roads of our lives. We must not be content with simply gathering facts about these roads, nor just cruising tourist-fashion down them in the hope of encountering some interesting experience.

For people who spend their lives trying to help others face up to the journey of growth and healing, the distinction between knowing about self as opposed to knowing self becomes crucial. Many people undergo self-reflective exercises ranging from "reflective" prayer to intensive psychotherapy. Yet this self-exploration may never get beyond an informational level. Like the tourist who never gets out of the automobile to feel the earth beneath his feet, such people refuse to face the risk of truly recovering the original chapters of their story. They amass many facts about their psychological reality but acquire very little of the practical wisdom that contains the real key to healing and growth. After much effort to explore the early roads of their life, they are still strangers in their own locality. Anyone

involved in spiritual and psychological healing seeks
ways to overcome this frustrating tendency to settle for
mere information instead of discovering liberating self-
knowledge.

The solution offered here may appear to be simplistic and naive. It is based upon a firm belief that growth
and spiritual healing have not been invented in our day.
For centuries people have been growing in wisdom and
authentic self-knowledge. To discover the source of this
wisdom we must return to the fundamental reality of
what healing entails. Healing, in its most radical expression, involves re-establishing broken relationships and
restoring life-giving communication. The human heart
is not healed by inundating it with sophisticated facts
about the human condition. Accumulating information
is a recent phenomenon. Communicating through the
medium of story has been with us since the dawn of
human consciousness.

The human heart is not a computer, and programming it with appropriate facts in the hope that it will
select a healing course of action seems to be a futile exercise. The heart is as old and as wise as the human
race. It is the source of life, of mystery, and of creativity.
To expect this exquisite creation to yield up its liberating story through the medium of abstract facts is a vain
hope indeed. Only the magic of a story can capture the
real adventure of our unique journey in life. Our journey, told as God's special story about us, gives a meaning and a purpose to our road in life that no scientific
analysis could ever accomplish. This is the difference between a journey that increases feelings of alienation and
frustration and a journey that generates intimacy and
purpose. The difference lies in whether or not we have
developed the capacity to hear God telling us our story
for the journey.

On the road to Emmaus two disciples of Jesus met a stranger. They told this stranger the story of the events that had taken place just prior to their leaving Jerusalem. Then the stranger, in his turn, illuminated their story by a story of his own. In doing so he transformed their journey into a profoundly spiritual experience. As a result of this transformation their steps were lightened and their hearts were lifted. "Did not our hearts burn within us as he talked to us on the road and explained the scriptures to us?" (Lk 24:32). The burden of our journey will be lightened if we too listen to the stranger's story within us on our journey to Emmaus. Our journey will take on a new purpose and a new direction if we can learn to recognize the abiding presence of God in our hearts and in our lives. Walking in the company of God and listening to his good news is the only authentic way of "shortening the road."

Any journey can become irksome if we do not know how to shorten it creatively. So too with our journey in life. God has given us a way to lighten our steps and lift up our hearts. When we reach the end of the back road that leads to our home, we do not go on further. We invite Jesus to stay with us in our house — which has always been his house — because the story will continue.

Old houses, mansions, and castles always attract visitors. We are attracted by the story of the house even more than by its stones or mortar. The story may be so important that the house can be demolished and disappear and yet we visit the site and relive the story. Often in Ireland as a boy I would come upon a tourist gazing into an empty field. On inquiring if I could be of some assistance he would point to an exact spot in the field, and tell me of the house that had stood there, the house where his grandfather was born and reared before he emigrated to a foreign land.

One thing that will entice us down the significant back roads of our life is the realization that the house waiting to receive us has a very interesting story. Once we realize that within us we bear a story of unique value and interest, we get the courage to make that interior journey and reclaim our house. But if we fail to appreciate the story of our house, then there is little chance of our being sufficiently enthusiastic to make the journey.

There are three possible attitudes to the story of our house. Each attitude will determine the quality of the journey we are prepared to undertake. First, there is the non-reflective attitude, usually formed on the fast highways of our life. A convenient story has been formed that rationalizes our obsession with speed and efficiency. This might be termed a "cover" story of our life. It is not our true story but it serves a useful purpose. It convinces us that only the main roads of our life have meaning and significance, even though these roads will not lead to a house that can be called a home. This story, which corresponds to the false self, dismisses as irrelevant anything that does not reinforce the journey on the main roads. It despises detours and the back roads that lead to our true home. Sadly, there is no interest in recovering the true story that opens up our heart to the restorative action of God.

Second, there is the conventional attitude of the tourist. The back roads have been explored and the interesting house has been reached. An impersonal guide provides an informative tour by remaining faithful to the official story. The tour is professionally competent and gives good value for the entrance fee. The tourists are satisfied and ready to visit more sights. For some people the exercise of counseling or psychotherapy works in this way. Much information has been gleaned and a tour has been completed. But the experience has been

impersonal and the real story of the house remains un-
recovered. Tourist and house remain strangers, and the
house reveals no transforming secret.

Third, we may be introduced to the house and recover
its real story through a guide who sincerely loves the
house. I remember on one visit to France, the French con-
freres of my religious congregation were quite friendly
with a family who lived in a very historical chateau. I
was invited by the family to visit this beautiful house.
The lady of the house took me on a guided tour through
the chateau. Her husband's ancestors had lived there for
hundreds of years. She was truly in love with the chateau
and had begun restorations in an abandoned wing. The
lady knew the story of the house so well that it came
alive. This was a journey of celebration and sincere love,
so different from my other experiences of guided tours
where the house was simply an object of curiosity.

God knows our house so well that he alone possesses
the real and authentic story. A journey through our
house in the company of God will bring our house alive.
Many areas may be in dire need of repair. Nevertheless,
the special story told by God will cast an enchantment
over our whole house. It will never appear the same
again. Its true story has been recovered and we are invited to celebrate it. We have only to devote our energies to learning how to listen to our real story for the
interior journey to begin. But this is a matter for the
next chapter.

We might do well to remember that the art of sto-
rytelling is not instantly acquired. It demands years of
practice in the company of a good storyteller. The following incident underlines this truth.

A tourist entered a public house in a tiny village in
Ireland and witnessed what he considered to be most
unusual behavior. Each villager took it in turns to shout

out a number, then the rest of the crowd erupted in loud laughter. The tourist inquired of the barman what was going on.

"In this village we are so familiar with all the funny stories that we assign each of them a number and this dispenses with the need of repeating them," said the barman.

The tourist decided to have a go. He shouted out a number. There was a deathly silence. He shouted out another number, again there was no response.

He asked the barman, "What am I doing wrong? Are the stories not funny?"

"Well," replied the barman, "the stories are great, but it is the way you tell them!"

Reflection Exercises

1. Spend a few minutes imagining your life in terms of a unique story.

— Recall some of the incidents from your life that would provide exciting ingredients for a story.

2. Identify people in your present or past who helped you to appreciate the uniqueness of your story.

3. Ask God for the grace to grow into a greater appreciation of your story so far.

3

Listening to the Story

One day a country woman was walking along a back road near her home when she came upon a lady tourist in severe distress. It seemed that this woman had been exploring some of the back roads in the area on foot and had become hopelessly lost. She was now thoroughly disoriented and panic-stricken. The local lady brought her home, made her some tea, and listened sympathetically to an incoherent outpouring in a foreign language. She was able to work out the husband's whereabouts and contacted him. He could speak English, and as he thanked the local woman, he told her that his wife had ceased to panic the moment she realized that she was in the company of a lady who could understand French. The local lady replied with a smile, "I'm afraid, sir, I am not familiar with any foreign languages. My schooling was very limited."

This simple story illustrates a very profound truth. The gift of listening transcends all barriers of race, social class, and language. This type of listening instantly reaches the heart of a person. Obviously, the local woman in the story possessed this gift in abundance, so much so that the distressed lady thought her new-found friend could understand French. God desires this type of listening in order to enable us to hear his story. It is often referred to as the "art of reflective living."

Acquiring this art involves developing the capacity to connect appropriately with our interior world and learn the language of the heart by listening to God speaking in our everyday experience. The process will enable us to hear the real story of our journey being unravelled from our past to illuminate our present and our future. So let us now briefly review some of the suggestions made by wise people who promote the art of reflective living.[4]

The first thing we need to do is to *slow down*, to cultivate a slower rhythm in our daily lives. This might sound like trivial advice, but let me assure you that it contains deep wisdom. Many of us today lead dangerously hectic lives. In general, we move too fast. Our physical health can be affected by the frantic pace of our everyday living, and our spiritual well-being can be harmed as well. The pace of our life is such that listening to the real needs of our human and spiritual condition is almost impossible. The technological age has invaded our everyday experience and now sets the pace of our lives. In effect, we unconsciously model ourselves on the machine.

In our grandparents' day the machine was confined to restricted areas such as factories. On the whole people tended to pace their lives according to *living* models of movement — the canter of a horse, the stride of walking, the flow of a river, the flight of a bird. With little mechanistic efficiency to help them, waiting patiently became a normal feature of their lives. People were more tranquil, more present to each other, and more attuned to the sensitive movements of their hearts. I suspect we have all come across people who have not been programmed by our hectic technological pace. I meet many people in Africa who bring me back to this slower rhythm of living, even though I do not always appreciate having to slow down my ingrained hectic expectations.

Today, many of us feel that patience is no longer necessary. The convenience of an automobile, the ready availability of telephones and computers, the global immediacy of television and air travel have so raised our expectations of instant results that patience is seen as a rather quaint virtue. It seems most unreasonable to be asked to live within the limiting boundaries of our struggling humanity. Today, we are literally reaching for the stars.

This high level of expectation must have a deleterious effect on our spiritual and human growth.[5] As we wait, in an airport lounge for a delayed flight, in a traffic jam, in a long line at the supermarket check-out, or even while waiting for the elevator to arrive, what goes on inside of us? Our blood pressure and many other physiological concomitants of stress are continually activated. The physical state of our body has been conditioned by this hectic style of living. But the psychological effects of this conditioning constitute an even greater threat to our humanness. Because we have such a high level of expectation of mechanical efficiency, we perceive all delays as serious obstacles. We react by becoming hostile and aggressive. Unfortunately, this state can become chronic, hidden beneath a carefully developed exterior calm. It can even destroy our vital moments of relaxation and recreation.

This psychological condition of aggressive hostility will damage the quality of our relationship with ourselves and with other people. It will also damage our relationship with God. How can our hearts be nurtured and sensitized if we regard them as efficient pumps in a machine? How can we grow in authentic self-love and wisdom if our self-reflections are more akin to an instruction manual for engineers rather than to a living story longing to be told? Listening to the heart and with the heart becomes impossible. Our presence to ourselves, to God, and to others becomes severely restricted.

To extricate ourselves from this mechanistic style of behavior requires certain deliberate decisions on our part. First, we must examine our consciousness in order to determine the degree of our enmeshment in this behavior. Then we must learn to switch off this mechanistic style whenever an opportunity presents itself. We must realize two things: first, that the habit of behaving in a mechanistic manner may have become deeply ingrained and will call for regular practice at slowing down; second, that results will be slow in coming since the body is a slow but sure learner.

Another requirement for reflective living is to reconnect with a deeper order in reality. This order predates the machine and has been carefully designed by God to *nurture life*. Because of the hectic pace of our everyday living, this sacred order has been submerged beneath a highly functional approach to life. Instead of a welcoming response to its life-giving demands, we often display a blind, angry reaction because of the need to submit to the laws of this fundamental order. A story will better demonstrate the difference between these two approaches to God's basic order in life.

In a remote part of a large country a traveler arrives at a stream. He is extremely thirsty. On entering the stream he sees that the water is very muddy and becomes enraged. He realizes that a herd of buffalo has entered the stream further up. He curses the buffalo and angrily beats the surface of the water in the hope that the mud will be dissipated, but the action only stirs up more mud from the bed of the stream. In a fit of exasperation, he storms off in search of another stream.

A second person, a native to the area, arrives at this muddy stream. He also wishes to drink from the water and quench his thirst. He notices the muddy condition of the stream, but he is glad. He now knows that the buffalo have returned to the area and are refreshing themselves in the stream. He knows that the buffalo will soon move on to graze, and that the mud will settle back into the bed of the stream. So he sits and waits patiently for the stream to be restored for his use. He is grateful to the god of nature for being so generous to all life in that area.

This story illustrates very vividly the difference between a reactive style of living and the welcoming response of an authentic reflective style of living. I say authentic here because there is a type of reflection that does not touch this deeper order of God. People sometimes say that they are seriously reflecting when in reality they are trying to work out some functional problem. This form of cogitation is exercised at a superficial level whereas authentic reflection transcends the cares of our possessive ego and searches for an ordering of reality beyond our immediate control.

God has arranged an order in creation that is geared toward promoting life. This will obviously be a different order from the kind that is designed to maintain a machine or regulate our functional concerns. In order to reflect on some preliminary notions of this order, let us recall a few characteristics of that reality it serves — life.

As our story makes clear, we share life with other living creatures. The interdependency, designed by God, between all levels of life must be regarded as a sacred bond uniting all living things. A valiant effort is being made today to heal the rift that has arisen between ourselves and God's dynamic presence in all creation. Seeking to develop a creation spirituality is an honest attempt to restore the essential reverence for God in nature that was lost in our obsessive drive to control the forces of our planet.[6] Spectacular accomplishments in human technology may have led us to exaggerate our place in the order of nature, and lessened or even destroyed our awareness of the bond that God established between us and our environment.

Life is vulnerable and, at times, powerless. This demands of us a gentleness and sensitivity toward the painful struggle of the growth process. It also demands of us a great patience with the mysterious phenomenon of growth and development. As highly rational creatures we have the capacity to deal with reality in abstract terms. This removes the particular reality from its *lived* context as well as its particular growth process. We create an idealized version of reality, a highly dangerous state. Viewing life from a strictly logical and abstract perspective robs it of its real struggles and embodied reality. When we view ourselves purely from the intellect, we engage in the debilitating exercise of *introspection*. This impoverished manner of viewing ourselves has nothing to do with the type of reflection that reveals God's story.

Life is not as chaotic and as haphazard as it sometimes appears. A hidden and significant set of laws governs life in all its variety, nursing it toward greater fulfillment of its potential. Even in what appears to be turmoil and meaninglessness, a deeper law of growth is at work. This is especially true of the higher processes of life such as spiritual and human growth. As a child I was always impressed by my parents' unshakable belief that there was a divine order of things governed by "God's blessed will." I know that blind adherence to what is claimed to be the will of God can sometimes be a simplification of reality, indicative of an unhealthy passivity. In my parents' case, however, it seemed to have the opposite effect. In the painful and often baffling ordeals they both had to endure through the loss of children, property, and health, they steered their lives directly into the full force of the gale on their journey. They never wavered but kept going, knowing that the shape of their journey made sense to God, however limited their view of the road. But they also knew that eventually they would reach a sheltered area on the road and be allowed to rest for a while. In that moment of trustful reflection they could detect the contours of God's movement in their life, however dimly. The simplicity of their trust in a divine purpose behind their experiences was shared by most of the people of that time. It would seem that as people moved further into the technological age, their capacity for this kind of faith and trust declined.

Another feature of authentic reflective living is the ability to stay with an experience in order to discern its deeper meaning. The obvious model for this kind of reflection is to be found in the gospels, with Mary, the mother of Jesus. Whenever she was presented with a mysterious turn in her road, she did not react impulsively. If the event was too challenging and the experience too complex to be quickly assimilated, she waited. She stored these mysteries in her heart and gently submitted them to a patient review. She knew that there was a deep divine purpose to life and patiently waited for the deeper order of reality to emerge.

This ability to dwell with an experience is an essential element in contemplation. In pretechnological cultures many people with no particular spiritual training had a natural ability for contemplation. In our highly technical age, this skill is not easily cultivated. Our technological achievements have intensified our hunger for power and control. This tends to inhibit one of the most important qualities for a contemplative style of living. To be truly contemplative we must be able to stay with reality as it presents itself and resist all urges to try to manipulate it. Unless a situation reasonably demands action, the only creative response is one that calls for great patience and a willingness to stay with the experience until a deeper meaning emerges.

We can respond creatively to many ordinary experiences in our lives, thus developing in ourselves the art of living. For instance, can we recall the taste of our last meal, our first encounter with the world this morning, the smile on our friend's face, and other such significant moments which connect us with God in our daily life? Such experiences are often programmed out of our consciousness by our hectic and reactive style of living. I believe, however, that many of the people who graced my early life had the ability to dwell with ordinary experiences. Our house was generous in offering a cup of tea to passing strangers. I distinctly remember one lady who relished most graciously a friendly cup of tea. She lingered over the taste in such a way that the impression of her enjoyment is still with me. Other vivid memories are of my mother at the kitchen window in the twilight of an evening gazing peacefully at the slowly fading countryside, or of my father resting on a shovel in the garden, gazing into the distance.

These were probably moments of great sacredness, when the only response necessary was a gentle dwelling with reality as it rested in the palm of God's hand. We need these sacred moments in order to feed our spirits and honor our place in reality. We should use a spare moment, or make one if need be, in which to practice this art of dwelling with an experience. Sit quietly and register what is happening around you. Do not try to manufacture a sacred moment. Just be *present* to what is happening before you. If this is too vague, then find some tranquil scene and stay with it for a short while.

It could be water flowing from a fountain, trees sway-
ing in the breeze, snow falling from the sky, a butterfly
tentatively seeking a resting place.

Many moments of potential spiritual richness are offered to us throughout the day, but we often miss them,
perhaps because these moments may be experiences of
powerlessness that aggravate our reactive style of behavior. With practice and attention, we can turn the
time trapped in a traffic jam or waiting for an air flight
into a loving and friendly encounter with reality instead of using these moments to reinforce our corrosive
aggressiveness.

Functionally idle moments should serve rather than
annoy us. As we immerse ourselves in a world of high
technology our heads become the analytical center of
our consciousness wherein we try to process all the experiences that come at us during our waking day. God
wants us to assimilate *some* of these experiences as part
of our growth process. But this can be done only if we
switch off our functional approach to life and allow other
dimensions of ourselves to become active. We need a
period of time, especially toward the end of the day, in
which we can unwind and allow our feelings and impressions to catch up with us. This is a time to be alone
with oneself, with God, or with a special friend who allows us to retreat to a less functional, less hectic level of
being. This is the time when experiences that we suppressed or otherwise failed to deal with because of our
fast pace may be acknowledged or addressed. The process of assimilation works slowly. If we do not make
allowances for this process, imagine how many experiences have to be stored in our subconscious at the end of
each day. Is it any wonder then that many people have
difficulty sleeping at night? How many undigested experiences must be there after a number of years!

God speaks to us through our daily experience. He honors the fullness of his creation and communicates through the whole of our personhood. He does not collude with our reactive style of living by confining himself to our intellect or to our functional level of behavior. God will try to coax us off the fast highways of life and on to some quiet back roads, secluded places where he can speak more freely and reveal to us the full extent of his good news for us. Reflective living is essential if we are to be receptive to God speaking in our hearts. Only through this style of living are we in a condition to hear the story.

Finally, another important aid to developing a reflective style of living is to share with a trusted companion. Any sharing that frees us from our business transactions is excellent. Many people belong to groups of various kinds and this is to be encouraged, but here I will confine myself to a discussion of personal sharing. A special companion for the journey may be drawn from many different walks of life. It could be a marriage partner, a trusted friend, a spiritual director, a counselor, or merely an acquaintance who finds it easy to lend you an ear. God will use different people at different times. Some he will use more than others, so don't change a friend simply because you have been confiding in this person for a long time. The role of the person is less significant than the quality of his or her presence. By their nonintrusive presence and welcoming attitude such companions allow you to see, hear, and experience your real self. Some will have received training in this type of presence. Many more will possess this gift by instinct. In my own experience some of the best listeners have received no formal training whatsoever while some formally trained people have a poor ability to listen with their hearts and reflect our real concerns.

These special companions are in the direct service of God. Through them, God listens to us and reflects our deeper self-knowledge. God asks only that these people be open to their own journey and story if they are to be authentic mentors. Such people become mirrors in which we can see our real selves. And when we grow in the capacity to see our real selves, we learn to see God.

We have been reviewing some of the means by which we can cultivate the important skill of reflective living. If we enter into this type of presence to ourselves, to others, and to the world, then God will have little difficulty in getting us to listen to our story. The stranger on the road is vital to this development. Unfortunately some of the official guides in our life may know nothing about the way a mentor can mirror one's real self. This little story illustrates the difficulty we may encounter in trying to share our real selves.

Once upon a time, before mirrors had been introduced into personal use, a woman found one for sale in the market. The merchant showed her how to use it. She brought it home and, realizing that she was the only woman in the village who had one, she carefully hid it in her bedroom. At regular intervals through the day she would visit the room, take out the mirror, and admire herself. Her husband became very suspicious. She had tidied herself up a lot and no longer seemed to have any interest in him. All her interest seemed to be directed toward something hidden in the bedroom.

One day while his wife was away the husband searched the bedroom and found the mirror. To his horror, all his suspicions were confirmed. When he looked at it he discovered that it was the picture of a man. He decided that this was a matter for the priest. Only the priest could help him deal with this situation.

He went to the priest and told him the whole story. He showed him the proof of his suspicions, the picture of a man. The priest took the mirror and studied the picture. "Ha! Ha!" he said. "We'll have no trouble finding this rascal. He has the ugliest face ever seen on any man."[7]

Reflection Exercises

1. Decide on a program of relaxation that suits your temperament and situation. Try to stay faithful to the exercises on a daily basis.

2. Find a person with whom you can review your life on a regular basis, if you have not already done so.

3. Devote at least twenty minutes toward the end of each day to quietly reviewing your day. Some people find that keeping a journal of these reflections is helpful, but this is not absolutely necessary.

4. Ask God for a share in Mary's gift of reflective living.

4

Seeing the Road Ahead

Once a group of tourists got hopelessly lost among back roads. At last they encountered a local inhabitant and tried to get directions to the main road. Although he did his best, one of the angry tourists could not resist this parting comment. "Since coming to this country of yours we have met nothing but idiots. But you beat them all!" "That might be so, sir," replied the local man, "but I am not lost!"

The story suggests that expertise in particular situations is not always appreciated. This may be because we have a restricted understanding of "expertise" and, as a consequence, our appreciation of the challenge of certain situations may be likewise restricted. Our local guide was able to direct the tourists out of the maze of back roads and back on to the main highway, but how many people in the world today would appreciate this as a skill? Most people are impressed by such expertise as working with computers, flying an airplane, or performing a surgical operation. And yet, is not an ability to know by heart the intricate network of back roads something to be appreciated in its own right? The question we might reflect on is this: If this particular skill is not generally appreciated in our world today, are there other skills that are also being ignored? For instance, some people, insignificant in the world's eyes, possess a *wisdom* of inestimable value. But we pass them every day without so much as a glance.

The gift of wisdom was very much appreciated in the past. It is less appreciated today because of the availability of so many experts and specialists in particular fields. Wisdom is not a specialist gift, confined to a definite category such as morphology or carpentry. It is more diffuse and tends to permeate the whole of one's life. There is no specialized course of study or designated center offering tuition in this area. Wisdom can be learned only from constant exposure to the buffeting of experience on the back roads of life, roads that must be traveled without maps or signposts.

The word *wisdom* comes from the Latin word *videre*, "to see." It has a lot to do with seeing what is essential in life, for example, the order God has established in the world to nurture life, or the path he has laid down for each of us to become the person he has called us to be. Sometimes we realize with a start that someone in our midst with very little formal education, someone not rated highly by the world, is able to see clearly something the world cannot see. In the midst of the confusion of roads competing for our attention, they are able to recognize the path that leads to God. This kind of seeing is the wisdom buried in our hearts, the wisdom we must begin to recover if we want to see our road ahead of us. Since growth in wisdom is lived and experienced rather than analyzed or speculated upon, it is difficult to describe or define it. A story may be more helpful as a first step in demonstrating its existence.

I went on a pilgrimage to the Holy Land a few years ago. A day was set aside for an experience of the desert. An air-conditioned bus drove us to the edge of the desert, which was conveniently marked by a large hotel.

Here we were presented with our first option. Those who wished to have their desert experience indoors could do so in the comfort of the hotel lounge which looked out onto the desert. Those who wished to brave it outdoors walked about a quarter of a mile out to a very prominent monument erected by the Israelis to commemorate the 1967 Arab-Israeli war. Once there we were presented with another option. We could remain in the shade of the monument or fan out alone in different directions for forty minutes of meditation. On no account was anyone to wander too far from the watchful eye of the guide.

As I sat on a rock fighting back the fear of desolation, I saw a Bedouin woman on a donkey passing by a short distance away. She seemed to appear out of nowhere. I watched her as she weaved her way through the small sand dunes and headed out into the limitless desert before her. She made no attempt to check her bearings with the monument. As she became a tiny black speck on the horizon, the daring of her journey hit me. Before moving back to the security of the monument I walked out to inspect the path, which I had presumed was capable of carrying this lady out into a frightening wilderness. All I could see were faint hoof-prints fading rapidly into the shifting sands. Soon there would be no trace of the Bedouin woman on the donkey.

Later that evening, on the bus bringing us back from the desert, I spoke to the driver, who was familiar with the Bedouin way of life. I was intrigued to know how she could travel through the desert without the aid of a path. He simply said, "But she can see a path."

We live in a world that offers many artificial adventures. We can have the experience without the hardship that was once an integral part of the adventure. We can be transported to the Holy Land in comfort, in a matter of hours. In days gone by this same journey might have taken a lifetime. The wilderness of the desert can be viewed from a hotel lounge! When we do venture outside the hotel, and gingerly explore the edge of this wilderness, we remain cosseted within the shadow of a gigantic man-made monument to ensure maximum protection against a few yards of rock and sand. Intellectually we know a great deal about the desert. It is neatly catalogued in our magnificent libraries. Yet who among us can reclaim the ancient skill of crossing a desert alone and unaided? Who among us is impressed to realize that at one time our ancestors made such journeys frequently, long before modern navigational aids were invented? Today, if we came upon such a person, would we be impressed? Probably not! This astonishing skill, this ancient form of knowledge known as wisdom, would most likely be reduced to a quaint accomplishment of an insignificant Bedouin people on the remote fringe of our technological society.

Today our conventional knowledge has become so conceptualized and systematized that we can traverse the entire world in the comfort and security of a well-appointed study. We can return from adventurous expeditions in libraries and centers of learning with scarcely a speck of dust from the journey. Yet we, who are so well equipped with information, lack basic skills and knowledge possessed by those who may never step foot in a library or university. In listening to people struggling with basic human issues in their lives I sometimes uncover something rather strange. So many of these people have received all the benefits of our modern educational systems, yet they are poorly informed about fundamental laws of ordinary and everyday experiences.

This is not to say that countless people who, for various reasons, have been catapulted out of their intellectual security into an uncharted desert of a terrifying experience — the loss of a loved one, of health, of job, of reputation, or simply of nerve — in a quiet and unassuming way, with no specialist help, manage to find their path in life again. Such people develop a wisdom that is simply a knowledge of the journey developed on the journey itself. Sadly, it often goes unappreciated because it is usually developed in situations which are beyond the superficial comprehension of our technological age.

Several aspects of our society are obstacles to the cultivation of wisdom. First, we have a tendency to over-conceptualization. We live in a world that has succeeded in harnessing many of the forces of our planet. Our advances give evidence to a highly cultivated functional capacity and a highly developed possessive ego. As we will see, this kind of development caters only to one dimension of our being. The educational system that promotes this type of character formation tends to ignore any areas of our being that do not directly promote technological progress. To increase the power of the intellect, everything is directed toward abstraction, intellectualization, and a focus on conceptual order. Other human capacities tend to be ignored, such as imagination and intuition. Our present cultural and spiritual poverty stems from excessive use of an isolated intellect. God intends this wonderful gift of our intellect to be used in harmonious cooperation with other vital capacities. It is no mere coincidence that children, before being put through our modern educational machine, possess these qualities of imagination and intuition in abundance. It is sad to realize that in submitting our children to an intensive exposure to conceptualization, we are stunting other capacities which would enable them to see the world in a holistic manner.

Second, we rely too much on experts. In our world of modern conveniences, experts are always readily available. By cultivating experts, the tremendous surge in development was made possible. A too ready access to an expert, however, can rob us of certain hidden gifts that contribute to the cultivation of wisdom. An elevator might be a great gift to people who have long stairways to climb or who suffer from some physical disability. If we use an elevator all the time, however, we lose an opportunity for healthy physical exercise. In like manner, if someone does our thinking, searching, and discerning for us, we lose the capacity to engage life courageously. We must be very cautious before turning over our lives, or certain elements of our lives, to people who are only too willing to take charge. In all matters that have a bearing on our personal growth and development, we must invest a generous amount of energy in prayer and heartfelt searching before turning to an expert. And even then, we must guard very carefully against being taken over. We use the expert to clarify options but retain the sacred exercise of decision for ourselves.

Another area in which the challenge to develop wisdom can be taken away from us is in too great a reliance on institutions and/or organizations. I specifically mention institutions here because of the considerable number of people I meet from religious backgrounds who have poor personal autonomy or capacity for discernment. Being trapped into institutional thinking, however secure it might feel, can rob us of the oldest gift of the human family, the ability to see the path with the eye of our own heart and to have the courage to follow it.

We have also lost the ability to listen creatively. Among very wise helpers and professional listeners creative listening is described as "listening with the third ear." This is listening with the ear of our heart, a skill not easily described. It has something to do with reflective living. It involves seeing a person not as a machine with buttons to be pressed but as a sacred world in which one struggles to bring God's order out of a temporary chaos. Each of us has the wisdom and the capacity to allow God to bring about order in our turbulent lives. We do not need other people to put our world together according to their designs — however neat their personal order may be. But we do need the support, the space, and the freedom to tour our chaotic house in the company of a compassionate friend and try to see the design for ourselves. In this listening exercise we can be certain that God is with us, because he has already begun this restorative and healing task.

In his book *The Little Prince*, Antoine de Saint Exupéry devised a small test in order to determine who had real understanding of life.[8] It was a drawing of an elephant inside a boa constrictor. To people young in heart, who still saw life through the eyes of wisdom, it was easy to identify the living creatures involved. To others, the picture had no life. These people claimed that it was a hat. How do we explain the difference in perceptions?

As human beings we do not live in a vacuum. We try to relate to our environment, make sense of it, and learn to move in it as securely and as comfortably as possible. This is the ancient human process of adaptation. We learn how to exist in and relate to our world in such a way as to enhance our chances of survival. We develop a pattern of responses that mostly occurs unconsciously and automatically as the situation demands, in order to protect ourselves against potential threats to our well-being in the environment. To illustrate how important this is, let us consider the following example. If I were transported to a large and hostile jungle and abandoned there, it is doubtful I would survive. I would not have developed an adequate pattern of automatic responses to ensure my survival.

These responses are not just types of behavior and feelings. They are also ways of looking at the world, perceptual models by which we assess our environment. These perceptual models are so important that many people get involved in their formation — parents, teachers, political and religious leaders. The degree to which each of these agencies can fashion the way we look at the world is the degree of their control over us. I have very vivid memories of incidents in my childhood in which my parents worried about "strange ideas" that I had picked up. The only thing strange about them was that they were slightly different from the ideas accepted in my home. My parents lost no time in hammering my perceptual models back into shape. My parish priest was likewise very concerned about a friendship I had with a boy of a different religious persuasion. He was afraid that this boy would fill my head with "funny ideas." This priest was concerned that my perceptual models would lose some of their traditional Catholic shape and that if this happened he might lose me.

We must never underestimate the power of early perceptual models. They are often reinforced in situations where control rather than authentic growth is promoted. Sadly, for some of us, much of our education and formation, both secular and religious, was geared toward reinforcing simplistic ways of seeing the world. This happened especially if these ways of perceiving reality also reinforced a particular agency's power and control over us. Approval was dependent upon our conforming to what was presented as the correct way of seeing things. These perceptual models gradually became enmeshed with our early identity and underpinned the false self.

This may explain why prejudices and biases can be so passionately defended. When our belief systems or perceptual models are attacked we mistakenly think that we are being personally attacked. Some of us reach adulthood and even old age still influenced by crude perceptual models that persist from an earlier age in spite of having received a good conventional education. A formation process with a strong emphasis on authentic growth and development seems required to eradicate the inaccurate elements of our perceptions. This formation does not necessarily take place in a formal educational setting. Some people who received very little formal education in their earlier years manage to refine their way of viewing the world and allow themselves to be formed in God's image. Perhaps they were exposed to challenging experiences that showed up the inadequacies of their early perceptual models.

We will return to this subject later but I have introduced the issue of perceptual models here in order to illustrate how our conventional education systems may reinforce these crude ways of seeing the world. Where this is the case, wisdom has little chance of being cultivated. If we regard wisdom as the capacity to see the world very close to the way God intends us to see it, then we can understand why unchallenged perceptual models are the enemy of wisdom. A readiness to be challenged about our perceptual models opens us up to truth and to God speaking to us in our experience.

While Jesus did not use the term *perceptual models*, nevertheless he was concerned about their power to obstruct his message. If I am in the grip of unchallenged ways of seeing the world, then I am blinkered and blind. Jesus referred to this type of blindness and the extent of its bad influence in the gospels. In Matthew we read, "The lamp of the body is the eye. It follows that if your eye is sound, your whole body will be filled with light. But if your eye is diseased, your whole body will be all darkness. If then, the light inside you is darkness, what darkness that will be!" (Mt 6:22–23).

We have been considering wisdom, what constitutes it and what obstructs its development. It has all to do with seeing with the heart. As the fox in *The Little Prince* so wisely said, "And now here is my secret, a very simple secret: It is only with the heart that one can see rightly; what is essential is invisible to the eye."⁹ The good news is that what is essential is right before our eyes, and wisdom enables us not to miss it, which reminds me of a story.

There was a very sharp custom's officer at a custom's post on the border between the Irish Republic and Northern Ireland. He had the reputation of being able to detect even the smartest attempts at smuggling. One particular case did give him considerable unease. Each day a man would arrive by bicycle, loaded down with parcels. Each day our custom's officer would make him open up all the parcels. Inside these parcels were old newspapers. The custom's officer was quite certain that he was missing something but after years of checking he never found anything.

Years later, after this officer had retired from the custom's service, he met his cyclist friend in a public house. They got talking over a drink. Finally, the retired custom's officer asked a straight question. "Mike," he said, "you were smuggling something — what was it?" "Bicycles," came the amused reply.

Reflection Exercises

1. Try to identify some insights that you have learned from experience.

— How many more insights can you learn from this kind of reflective exercise?

2. Try to become more conscious of your intuitive capacity when tackling problems. Check some of your reasoned decisions against your first intuitive hunch in order to reinforce this intuitive capacity.

3. How comfortable are you in *owning* your own decisions after prudent consultation?

4. When you next listen to someone, try to hear the message behind the words spoken. Also reflect back on some of your conversations in order to discern what you were really trying to say.

5. Are you able to identify certain perceptions about which you tend to become defensive? Are you willing to explore the background to these rigid perceptions in order to uncover a wider perspective on the situation?

6. Pray often for the gift of wisdom — "Lord, that I may see as you see."

5

Starting From the Right Place

I know of yet another tourist who was hopelessly lost and stopped to get directions from a local inhabitant. After explaining a manageable way through the maze of tiny roads in that area the local inhabitant could not resist making this final observation. "Of course, if I were in your place, I would not start from here at all!"

As can happen with apparently simple stories, there may be a depth of insight here into problems that can arise when we are invited to take a new road. We too often presume that all roads are the same and that all have similar starting places. Little do we realize that there are different starting places for certain roads and if we don't find them, we too will end up going around in circles. Are you confused?

Our tourist set out on a journey with a map, an automobile, and the presumption that all road systems were essentially the same the world over. In his present predicament he had unfortunately forgotten that once he left the main thoroughfares, his situation changed radically. The back roads and lanes belong to another way of life. They have served the intimate needs of the local inhabitants for centuries. They have a life of their own. They wander from one homestead to another with no sense of urgency but with an innate understanding of the intricate farm boundaries. On these tiny roads courtships were conducted, sometimes for many years, sometimes for a lifetime. Journeys to church, to school, to market, and to the graveyard were made on these roads. An intersection was nearly always a meeting-place for business and for recreation. So when a tourist stops and demands an instant key to this complex maze, any sensitive local inhabitant attempting to offer directions would surely worry about the tourist's access to this complex world.

A priest had been coming to see me about some personal difficulties. After a few meetings one thing became clear. He was experiencing a lot of difficulty in trying to find the right starting place for his journey. His difficulties were not unusual, but they had been bothering him for some time. He hoped to make a breakthrough to a level of his life where he would experience a bit more peace and confidence. He had tried all the usual spiritual remedies — retreats, spiritual direction, being prayed over at a charismatic prayer meeting. His story is an excellent illustration of an honest person struggling to find the right path in life, the path that will eventually lead him to his real home. A brief description of his attempts to start his journey may be a good way of introducing us to some key preparations for the journey to the heart.

He is a priest in his middle forties. For many years life was simply great. He can lay claim to many fine accomplishments. He has always been admired for his intellectual and organizational abilities. If he had not become a priest he feels sure that he would have been a success in whatever walk of life he adopted. Now at an age when he claims that he should know better, he is in a mess. He feels hopelessly lost and confused. He is inundated with feelings that he has not felt since he was a boy. He feels frightened because he has tried all the conventional helps that usually work for "sane and normal people" but do not work for him. He feels nothing but disgust and shame at himself. In a last desperate attempt to solve his problems, he is forced to come to me. Can I do anything to help?

If we stay with the imagery of the roads, his situation might be explained in the following manner. For some reason, as yet unknown, he has been sidetracked off his secure main road on to a back road that had long ago been abandoned. Being a man of exceptional managerial and analytical ability, he has come to expect that all problems in life can be submitted to a well-reasoned solution. Unfortunately, like so many of us, he is trapped into thinking that every resolution of a difficulty has the same starting point. He is conditioned to believe that the well-posted, well-lighted, straight highway is the only road worth traveling. Loitering on back roads is only for the mentally ill or for those who engage in unhealthy introspection. It is nice to go back to these roads in a nostalgic moment by recalling a memory or two, but to be lost there for any length of time is simply unbearable. These roads belong to a period of his life that is now well and truly behind him. God is now to be found on the modern highway, where the real action in life takes place. He has come to me for directions. How can he extricate himself from this nightmare of back roads and return as quickly as possible to the security and efficiency of his main road?

This is a crucial moment for this priest's journey of growth and spiritual development. He does not realize that he is being offered an invitation to a whole new level of freedom and growth. His crisis is really a graced event on his journey in life to which he may or may

not respond. He is being offered an opportunity to uncover the real self lying buried beneath the false self
to which he has grown attached. Since leaving childhood and adolescence, this man has succeeded in learning how to travel the main thoroughfares of life and he
now defines himself in terms of this success. The truth
is that this was only intended to be a temporary definition and to give a temporary sense of self. Once he had
become established in life, he should have gone back to
his earlier beginnings, to recover the authentic starting
place, and then journey toward the discovery of his real
self. Viewed from that perspective he should be thank-
ful that now he is being forced off his main road and
invited to befriend the back roads of his life once more.
He himself admitted in the course of one of our talks
that it has been a long time since he traveled these back
roads — not since childhood by his own account. He has
returned fleetingly as a tourist whenever he saw a play
or read a book that touched on his early childhood, but
apart from these brief detours, he has lost touch with this
early world. In fact, until his present troubles began, he
did not realize that it still existed. Now it has returned
to haunt him and seriously hamper his progress on the
busy route of his business affairs.

The priest's true situation would seem to be this. No
matter how fearful he may feel, he is not lost in some
hostile territory. He does not need to be rescued. He is
not a mere tourist in these parts in need of emergency
road services. As his temporary companion on the journey I must resist treating him as a lost tourist. I must not
direct him back to the false safety of his main road. He
belongs here. Though he doesn't realize it yet, he is the
local inhabitant in this situation. He used to live here.
But since he became so invested in the speed and the
power of the main roads, he has become a stranger to

these parts. But God, in the graced events of his present crisis, is calling him out of his superficial understanding of himself, the false self, back to the earlier roads of his journey, to those little roads where richer chapters of his story need to be heard. In this way he will begin to recover the full story of his journey and thereby gain a more authentic understanding of his real self.

If we reflect for a while on our own struggles, however great or small they may appear, we may find that we are not unlike this priest. Some of us are also eager to build secure highways through the unfamiliar areas of our lives. Once we have grown accustomed to these fast highways, we, too, are reluctant to move to a new starting place and relearn the directions for the back roads of our lives. We, too, feel lost and confused when, for whatever reason, we are forced to revisit these back roads. We hang on to the security and sense of identity provided by our main roads and even take pride in our false selves. When God intervenes through significant experiences in order to force us off this main road, how many of us welcome this crisis as an invitation to grow more fully into our real selves? How many of us believe that our unplanned detour is in fact a journey of liberation to a place where God is waiting to walk our roads with us again?

Jesus identified this starting place in a variety of words and images. At times it might be for him the heart of our lives. At other times it might be where we find the cross we must carry, the place where our human condition weighs more heavily. It may be where our greatest fears are. But in very vivid imagery Jesus identified this starting place as the child within us. It represents a stage of our journey that many of us believed had long ago been completed. It defies all logic and economy of travel when someone recommends that we return there or remain there if we have unwittingly blundered into it. Yet this is how God's law of healing and growth is applied. Before we go further, we must be fully alerted to a potential hazard on our journey. Why do we find the back roads of our lives so threatening? Why are we so ready to settle for the false comfort of the main roads?

It would seem that most of us are very uncomfortable with the human condition in general. This has something to do with our fear of the vulnerable, powerless, limited side of ourselves. As a result of this fear we have a very inadequate acceptance of our humanity, and this fragile acceptance breaks down whenever we are confronted with uncertainty, confusion, or delayed results. These are precisely what we encounter when we find ourselves on the back roads of our life. Instead of drawing on patience and compassion to handle these encounters, we treat them with rejection, oppression, and contempt. This is the root cause of most of our unhappiness. Because of the insidious tendency we have to reject ourselves, Jesus had to intervene in our history to restore within us the healing and redemptive act of self-acceptance.[10]

Whenever I explain the significance of self-acceptance in Christian spirituality I usually take a flower or a plant as the most exquisite example of this quality. Jesus himself was impressed with the simple trust of the flower in its own innate goodness. The flower totally accepts its "flowerness" in all its vulnerability and powerlessness. This unique combination of gifts and limitations constitutes the flower's originality and value. Therefore the flower is a compelling model for us who can freely decide to accept or reject the fullness of our humanity and unique value.

One day at a conference I was in the midst of a paean to a nearby plant when I noticed a distinct look of discomfort on the faces of the people near me. I stopped and enquired the cause of their discomfort. One person with some embarrassment told me that the plant in question was artificial. It was an excellent imitation of a plant but it was made of plastic. While waiting for the laughter to subside, I made a solemn resolution. In the future, before I addressed a flower or a plant, I would test whether it was real or not by surreptitiously digging my thumbnail into a leaf. If the plant is real, the leaf is slightly damaged and the life-juice of the plant is revealed. If the plant is false then the leaf is invulnerable and remains undamaged.

Here too we might find a helpful reflection for our lives. The authenticity of the flower or plant is determined by its vulnerability. In our lives, fear of vulnerability underlies all our self-rejection. If we listen again to the priest's story we will hear him say that he feels nothing but shame and disgust at himself. If we listen to people in emotional distress we eventually hear them voice deep-seated anger toward themselves. The basic source of this self-rejection is the shocking realization of the vulnerability of the human condition. When life is moving securely in the fast lane, there is an apparent self-acceptance. We might even claim with pride that we really like ourselves. In reality we like our accomplishments, our superficial self-image, and the many pleasurable sensations God has enabled us to enjoy. But when our dreams have been shattered, our projects have failed, and we lie powerless and confused, sinking deeper and deeper into despondency, we come to rest on the basic stuff of our human condition. This is what needs to be accepted. Unfortunately, this is what we tend to reject. Here the seeds of a corrosive self-hatred take root. This painful vulnerability is the characteristic feature of our humanity that most needs to be embraced in order to restore our human condition to a healed state.

This is the starting place for our journey of healing and growth.

This is how I understand the redemptive intervention of Jesus in our lives, how I understand the healing he came to provide. He came to teach us how to accept the full implications of our human state and how to take on the challenge of the back roads of our journey and see it through to the end. In taking on our human condition, Jesus tackled the insidious tendency toward self-rejection at its two-fold source.

First, there is what might be called a historical source of self-rejection cultivated in early life. By the mere fact that they are limited, fragile, and dependent, children remind us of a hateful side of our lives. Therefore we oppress in them what we would like to oppress in ourselves. Apart from criminal child abuse, even good parents can unwittingly generate in their children a subtle shame of their struggles and limitations. This is done in the mistaken belief that such shame will provide a greater incentive to excel. The message too often repeated is that power and efficiency are the mainstay of happiness and self-esteem. Areas of struggle and limitation are to be avoided at all costs. And when the child inevitably lingers or dallies on the back roads, he or she is often ungraciously dragged back to the more comprehensible and achievement-oriented main road. The lesson is not lost on the child. The sad rejection of his human condition has begun.

Second, there is what might be termed an endogenous source of self-rejection. This is found inside a person rather than being imposed from outside. It would seem to come from the very nature of the human condition. In short, it comes from our capacity to sin. This seems to be as close as we can get to a psychological description of original sin. Since we have the capacity to accept freely the unique reality of our created condition, we also have the capacity to reject it. And since an integral part of our unique reality is powerlessness and limitations, we can withhold our obedient acceptance of this reality. Instead we might look for a "tree of knowledge" as an alternative source of value and as an antidote to powerlessness and limitations. This act of rejection of God's arrangement of our human condition would seem to be very similar to the description in Genesis of our first parents' act of rebellion and original sin.

The way of life that Jesus came to offer us would seem to be the only way to heal this sinful rejection at its two-fold source. Jesus did not come into our lives only to reveal who God is. He came into our lives to also reveal us to ourselves.[11] He came into the heart of our humanity and took on the full burden of our struggles and weaknesses. While standing in our place he said the yes to God that our first parents refused to say and that we still find so hard to utter. In doing this, Jesus redeemed us all and opened up for us the real starting place for our journey of growth and development. This is a profound act of reconciliation with, and acceptance of, the full implications of our human condition.

While self-acceptance is the correct starting place, it must not be understood immaturely. When some people hear the expression "self-acceptance," they think that a permissive and irresponsible attitude is being promoted — license to do what they like provided it is done in a spirit of self-acceptance. Such an interpretation could not be further from the truth. Self-acceptance in the present context means that we have become reconciled with a starting point that will now inspire us to complete the journey designed for us by God. In finding the right starting place and accepting it in the spirit of Jesus, we are empowered to restore our house to the original plan of our Lord and Creator. Jesus saved us by inserting us back into the human process that unfolds God's original plan for us.

This understanding of redemption is beautifully illustrated in the temptations of Jesus in the desert. Jesus has been removed from the conventional immunity to his humanity by his stay in the desert. Fasting has further exposed the fundamental poverty of the human condition. He is weak and vulnerable. At this point the devil realizes the extent of Jesus' vulnerability. He constructs his temptations exactly in accordance with the weak state of Jesus. The subtlety of the devil's approach is amazing. Jesus is not tempted to become further enmeshed in his humanity as is often thought to be the nature of temptation. On the contrary, he is tempted out of his humanity and back into his godhead. He is offered gifts and status that confer power and invulnerability. These are the very elements we reach for as an antidote against the vulnerability of our human condition.

In being offered the power to turn a stone into a loaf of bread, Jesus is being offered a miraculous immunity to basic human needs. In being invited to force God to exercise his special protection toward Jesus by guarding him against the results of a fall, Jesus is being tempted to reach for a miraculous protection against his human fragility. By offering Jesus all the kingdoms of the world, the devil was tempting Jesus to eliminate from his humanity a healthy consciousness of powerlessness and dependency. If Jesus had succumbed to these temptations he would have left us, abandoning us to a perpetual war against our humanity and against the original plan of God for our development. By staying with us he offers us the real way, the real truth, and real life.

A very simple story underlines the dangers of self-rejection and the obstacle it presents to God's attempts to launch us on our journey.

Once upon a time there was an evil king who was very cruel to his subjects. One day he was killed in a hunting accident. He was succeeded by his younger brother who was a good and kind person. In order to begin his reign in a spirit of love for his subjects he decided to make a profound and public act of reconciliation with his people. Since he could not visit each person individually he asked his people to select the person whom they considered to be the lowliest in his kingdom as their representative. He would have supper in the home of this person as an expression of his wish to be close to his people in their humble situations. A poor widow who lived in a small cottage deep in the forest was selected. She was delighted with the honor but requested a little time in order to prepare for the coming of the king.

Days, weeks, and months passed by and there was still no sign from the widow that she was ready to receive the king. After investigating the cause of the delay the king discovered that the widow had enlisted the help of most of the people in the kingdom and they were now laying the foundations of a gigantic castle. It was reported that when this castle was finished, the poor widow would be ready to receive the king.

The king was hurt and frustrated by this response to his attempt at reconciliation. The king, although powerful in every other respect, was powerless to move closer to his people. He wanted to meet his people in their littleness and vulnerability, but they wanted to meet the king and start their journey of reconciliation from a position of power, control, and an idealized but false understanding of who they were.

The attitude of the poor widow is familiar to many of us. We may be willing to undertake a journey of reconciliation with God, but we want to control the conditions of the meeting and the place from which the journey starts. God wants to visit with us in our real house, the home he provided for us. We think that this home is a hovel because of its limitations and vulnerabilities. Therefore, we reject it and set out to establish our own pompous house, the home of the false self. We have the power to frustrate the deepest desires of God to meet us in our weakness and struggles. We want to grow into the person which God has called us to be on our terms. We do not want to start our journey from the right starting place.

In this chapter we have tried to emphasize the importance of finding the right starting place for our journey and accepting it in a true spirit of reconciliation and commitment. Here is a little story about a man who had a bit of trouble with his starting point.

One night a local villager was on his knees going around in circles under the only street light in his home village. When a visiting tourist asked him what he was doing, he said that he had dropped his wallet and was now searching for it. The tourist got down on his knees and he too began to search. After some time the tourist asked the villager if he was sure that he dropped it there. The villager said that he was not. "And where were you when you first missed your wallet," asked the tourist. "I was down one of those dark alleys," said the villager. "Well, why, in the name of all that is holy, are you looking for it here?" asked the tourist. "Well, you see, the light is much better here!" replied the villager.

Reflection Exercises

1. In a review of your life try to determine how compassionate you are toward yourself when you experience failure.

2. How often do you try to identify, in a spirit of gratitude to God, your special gifts and talents?

3. As a result of reflecting on your unique story and journey, are you trying to recover some of the joy and pride that God must feel for having created you?

4. Each morning and evening and whenever you become impatient with yourself, make a fervent act of acceptance of yourself before God.

5. Try to diagnose certain behaviors and attitudes that diminish your sense of self-worth. With the help of God's grace, make a decision to address this situation.

6

The Old and the New Road

One day a tourist asked a jarvey to take him from the railway station to the only hotel in the village. Now there are two roads to this hotel. One road, called the new road, is direct and therefore much shorter. The other, called the old road, meanders quite a bit and is therefore much longer. Since the weather was fine and the tourist was on vacation, the jarvey decided to take the old road.

After traveling for some time the angry tourist challenged the jarvey. "I want you to know that I have been here before and this is not the most direct route to the hotel. In fact we are going in the opposite direction!" "Not to worry, sir," replied the jarvey, "it will get us there in the end and will cost only a little bit more. On this road you never can tell who we might meet or what we might see. And sure, if we meet nobody or see nothing, no harm done. We will have all the more time to get to know one another."

This story highlights two very basic and radically different approaches to life. These two approaches have been described in various ways down through the ages. In the gospels they are exemplified by Martha and Mary. Antoine de Saint Exupèry, in *The Little Prince*, describes them in the first chapter and provides a test to help us determine which approach to life we adopt. Today, in our health conscious age, we talk about Type A and Type B behavior.[12] We also talk about approaches to life which are governed by different sides of the brain. For our purposes, we will call these two contrasting approaches the "way of the head" and the "way of the heart."

Each of these approaches to life has its own inherent value and purpose. If confined to their proper context, they are gifts to life and complement each other. Unfortunately, as many of us can testify from our daily experience, there is often great tension between these two ways. It would seem that people generally do not find it easy to discern which way is best suited for a particular situation. One person might think that the situation calls for quick and decisive action and would adopt the "way of the head." Another person wants to wait a while in order to see what develops. This would indicate the "way of the heart." In this chapter we will examine these two ways and briefly explore how they operate in everyday life.

Our opening story might help us to concretize our understanding of these two ways. Let us first take a look at the tourist and his perception of life. Obviously he is very invested in the shorter and more direct route. This route is both logical and economical in terms of time and effort. It is the most efficient way to achieve a concrete goal. The tourist is prepared to sacrifice sightseeing and friendly conversation in order to get to the hotel as quickly as possible. Even though he is on vacation and has scope to relax, he is still trapped in a way of relating to the world that unconsciously turns his vacation into a test of executive efficiency. He is not interested in a leisurely tour of the countryside. He is not open to meeting new people with whom he can have a heart-warming relationship. He shows no inclination to respond to the jarvey's invitation to share of himself. He does not hear or see the jarvey as a person but simply as an impersonal service — and a rather inefficient one at that. The tourist seems enraged that he has lost control over the situation and quickly moves to recover his power over the jarvey.

These characteristics, while out of place in a holiday situation, do have a purpose in the right context. In a situation in which certain results must be obtained in the quickest and most efficient way possible, the way of the head is by far the most desirable. In an operating room or on the flight deck of an airliner, these characteristics *must* be exhibited. The context demands a functional and efficient response. If an airplane is on the point of take off and the pilot engages in transcendental meditation instead of concentrating on the highly functional task at hand, the passengers would certainly have cause for alarm. As we describe some of the characteristics of this functional way of the head we will be able to assess which contexts are more suited to it.

A functional approach to reality is characterized by a marked division of labor and a strict separation of roles. This can be seen in any highly functional grouping of people — the military, the police force, and many other hierarchical organizations.

Since immediate results are the primary object of a functional exercise, strict control must be maintained at all times. There is strong emphasis on power and control in highly functional situations.

Individuals are submerged in roles. In a functional context, specific performance counts to the exclusion of all other dimensions of being. Anything that might take away from this performance has to be suppressed. The internal world is suppressed. We have only to think of the critical nature of the surgeon's or the pilot's task to appreciate the need for this type of emotional discipline.

A functional performance is essentially mechanistic. A compliment often attributed to a highly efficient team is that they operate like a well oiled machine.

Often the success of any functional operation depends on the correct assessment of the situation. A sharp assessment or diagnosis must be made. In this context being critical of procedures and performances is encouraged.

The rational must dominate. In order to ensure speedy results, a strict code of behavior or an agreed upon plan is always in place. To keep to this plan then our heads must be in control. If private feelings are allowed to influence performance, then the strict procedure could be interfered with.

Being valued according to the results produced, another key characteristic of the way of the head, is the most detrimental, because it may lead to people being devalued as the unique and sacred individuals they are created to be. A culture or way of life founded on this principle soon reduces people to units of production. When this particular characteristic is absolutized, the way of the head is activated whether the context requires it or not. This pulls us into a very hectic and anxious style of living.

In addition to these characteristics of the way of the head, you can surely think of many more, such as competitiveness, compartmentalization, and aggression. Two other features of this particular way also merit special mention. In a highly functional situation, the diminishment of the person is tolerated. War is an extreme example of this. Another characteristic feature of functional behavior is a narrowing of our perceptual range. Because of the urgency of the results there is a sharpening of focus in order to improve concentration. This can, however, prevent us from seeing the larger and often more creative picture.

It does not take much imagination to realize how damaging these characteristics can be in situations that do not require a strictly rational approach. Imagine the pain needlessly inflicted on children in a home that is too highly functional, or the impersonal atmosphere of a religious community that is run like an army barracks. Many areas must be assessed in order to determine the relevance of a particular approach to a particular context. We must remember that both as individuals and in community we can be trapped in an overly functional emphasis on the way of the head.

In marked contrast to the tourist, the jarvey has a totally different approach to life and embodies in a most gracious manner the way of the heart. For the jarvey, the *person* matters rather than the performance. In offering himself to the tourist as a potential friend instead of an impersonal operative, he is not worried about role assignments when two people have an opportunity to enrich their relationship with each other. The jarvey is invested in the *experience* of the journey rather than the efficient execution of a task. Judged from this perspective it is easy to understand why the jarvey would want to prolong the journey. He is not interested in controlling the situation or in perpetuating the illusion of power held by a self-important customer.

The way of the heart is fully invested in a growth approach to life rather than the production of immediate results. The context is completely different, found in a garden, in a nursery, in a caring home, in a religious development program, and in most counseling situations. In a growth context, if it is recognized as such, there is usually an implicit acceptance of a deeper and richer reality struggling to emerge from the present level of development. The seed will eventually produce a flower or plant. The helpless child will grow into a competent adult. A person in psychological or spiritual confusion will eventually find his or her way and generate a deeper and more mature level of being. What is essential in a growth situation is a nurturing relationship that realistically facilitates the dynamic unfolding of the growth process designed by God. Here is the work of a gardener as opposed to the work of a mechanic, the work of a parent as opposed to that of a commanding officer, the work of a counselor as opposed to the impersonal instructions of a computer. So let us now take a closer look at some of the characteristics of this way.

The context is one in which interpersonal relationships, not the correct order in a chain of command, are paramount. Divisions are eliminated and a community of people is cultivated. A person's value as an individual is emphasized.

Inspiration and motivation replace concern for power and control. In a growth context there is rarely a power struggle. People who have vision, enthusiasm, faith, trust, and the ability to motivate enjoy leadership positions.

Instead of concentrating on role, the over-all richness of the person is appreciated. Since there is no urgency to achieve immediate results, qualities other than functional efficiency can be celebrated.

Since authentic human growth begins in the heart, our interior world is cultivated. In fact, the inability to get in touch with our inner world frustrates the growth process. It is easy to appreciate how people immersed in the way of the head have shut off all access to their interior world.

Instead of a machine-like approach to life, a more welcoming and nurturing attitude is cultivated. Since life at a growth point is vulnerable and fragile, a gentle and sensitive approach is called for, although this does not rule out the need for firmness and discipline when authentic love requires them. A greater awareness of the process of growth must be promoted.

When we are in a critical situation, it is reasonable to demand a sharp assessment of the cause of the crisis and of the performance of the operatives. But when we are dealing with the growth process, such sharp judgments are not required. The experience of growth and the laws that govern it are less precise and exact. A greater allowance must be made for the stages of growth and the readiness to move from one stage to another. Sadly, in the moral and religious sphere, this Christ-like respect for the growth process is sometimes lacking.

In the way of the heart, the emotional dimension of experience is emphasized. This does not mean that the rational element is eliminated. This would be a most irresponsible way to promote emotional growth. But greater permission and scope are given to the recovery and the ventilation of feelings. In a later chapter this developmental approach to feelings will be further elaborated.

Having briefly reviewed some of the characteristics of the way of the head and the way of the heart, it becomes obvious that we wish to promote the latter growth approach to Christian spirituality and to avoid being unwittingly trapped in a functional and a disembodied approach to spirituality. From my limited experience of listening to people in their struggles to grow, it becomes evident that many of us are unable to relate to our inner world in a nurturing and growth-oriented way. We quickly adopt a functional approach and treat ourselves like a machine, an approach that is promoted by our prevailing culture. The frantic struggle to succeed and cope with a highly competitive world has generated the feeling that we are continually in a critical situation and are required to produce a crisis response. This gives rise to a hectic and reactive style of living. In order to cultivate a reflective style of living we must develop the ability to switch off the way of the head and switch on the way of the heart when and where the context demands it.

This type of conversion would be very dear to the heart of Jesus. But he was under no illusions as to how challenging this change of style really is. Jesus compared it to losing one's life in order to gain a deeper and more real life. Our investment in the functional way of the head is very heavy indeed. For one thing this particular approach is already dominant in our culture. It will not be easy to dislodge it. Apart from the force of habit, we also tend to hang on to it because the results of a functional approach are immediate and tangible, whereas the results of the growth approach are often vague, intangible, and long-term. In the way of the head, the rational dominates. Who does not appreciate clear-cut reasons and concrete plans? In the growth approach the heart often has reasons that the head finds very mysterious. The feeling of power and control that accompanies the functional way of doing things satisfies a deep-seated hunger in those who are struggling to come to terms with human vulnerability. In the growth approach we are made to face up to our vulnerability and weakness in order to integrate it into the wholesome experience of being human. This is an aspect of human growth not easy to sell in a culture obsessed with the machine.

In spite of these difficulties, attempts must be made to bring about a radical change in our behavior. So many neglected areas of our human condition cry out for the healing and growth offered by Christ. A Christian spirituality is incarnational in name only if it is overly influenced by the way of the head. Jesus clearly called for an abandonment of the ways of the world in order to establish an order of relationships in the service of real life. He could see clearly the insidious effects of a way of life that clamors for instant results and for more power and control. It is not difficult to identify some of these insidious effects at work in our society and connect them to the over-investment of our culture in the way of the head. War, class and race divisions, aggression, toleration of injustice, and oppression become the inevitable products of a hard, competitive, and acquisitive side of our humanity. True peace, healing, growth, wisdom, and an honest attempt to bring about the reign of God call for a different way more in tune with fostering life and love.

This is what St. Paul had in mind when he said,

> If I have all the eloquence of [humans] or of angels, but speak without love, I am simply a gong booming or a cymbal clashing. If I have the gift of prophecy, understanding all the mysteries there are, and knowing everything, and if I have faith in all its fullness, to move mountains, but without love, then I am nothing at all. If I give away all that I possess, piece by piece, and if I even let them take my body to burn it, but am without love, it will do me no good whatever.
>
> Love is always patient and kind; it is never jealous; love is never boastful or conceited; it is never rude or selfish; it does not take offense, and is not resentful. Love takes no pleasure in other people's sins but delights in the truth; it is always ready to excuse, to trust, to hope, and to endure whatever comes. Love does not come to an end (1 Cor 13:1–8).

In this chapter we have been underlining the importance of cultivating a more growth-oriented approach to life, which we have called the way of the heart. This emphasis on growth is not going to be universally appreciated. Some people have difficulty in seeing anything significant in the growth process. One little girl was clearly unimpressed by the whole business when approached by a lady tourist. This tourist had seen an exceptionally old man sitting outside his house. The little girl was playing nearby. "He must be a great age," said the tourist. "He is over a hundred years old," replied the little girl. "Why, that is amazing," said the tourist, "you must be very proud of him." "We don't think there is anything to be proud about with him," said the little girl. "He has done nothing else but grow old and he has taken an awful long time to do it."

Reflection Exercises

1. How machine-like are you in your approach to life? Check your approach against the characteristics of the way of the head. Do all your life-situations demand this approach, or do your need to change your aggressive approach to the world?

2. Can you identify any situation in your life that requires an approach by the way of the heart?

3. How comfortable are you with feelings? When did you last sit patiently with someone in emotional pain?

4. How are you progressing in your attempts to cultivate the art of reflective living?

5. Sit quietly with God for a short period each day and just rest in his healing presence.

Part 2

In Search of a Story ...

7

Coming Home

A little boy was sitting on the front steps of his home one day when a weary tourist arrived on foot. He had walked from the main road up a long winding lane and was exhausted. He slumped down beside the little boy and, with much exasperation, said, "It has taken me hours to get here. Why is that muddy lane between here and the main road so long?" The little boy replied, "Well, if it was any shorter, it wouldn't reach the house!"

This story highlights once again the central message of our last chapter. If we remain faithful to the old road we will eventually reach our destination. The road may be muddy and long, with many twists and turns, but it will take us to the front steps of our true home. Many of us, unfortunately, may be like the tourist. Our spirits may be weary because we have been caught up for too long in the throes of functional concerns. We have been seduced by the speed and efficiency of the new road. Now that we have to feel the ground beneath us and learn to tread its unassuming but muddy surface, we feel exasperated and discouraged. The good news is that if we keep faithful to this road and follow it to the end, we will arrive at our house. There we will recover important elements of our real self.

In the last chapter, the jarvey said something very significant about the old road. He said that traveling this road "will get us there in the end and will cost only a little bit more. On this road you never can tell who we might meet or what we might see. And sure, if we meet nobody or see nothing, no harm done. We will have all the more time to get to know one another." Let us now take a closer look at what our wise old guide might mean.

To the jarvey, who was open to growth and to listening to God in the stories of people's lives, a journey down the old road was relatively easy. Nevertheless, he realized that even for the most experienced traveler, it was a little more costly than traveling on the new road. The cost may be even greater for those with no experience whatsoever on the back roads of life. We may recognize ourselves in our tourist's reluctance to move away from the security of the new roads. But we may also realize at some deep level within us that we are missing out on a journey to areas of our life that are filled with meaningful and redemptive stories. And yet we resist the promptings of God's Holy Jarvey to take the longer way around. I wonder why this is so.

One possible reason may be found in the kind of experiences we could face on this road. For those of us who have built up our identity around the security of the fast roads, the slow and arduous pace of a back road offers too great a challenge to our self-understanding. If we see ourselves as logical, self-sufficient, efficient performers, then any experience that does not reinforce this impression becomes threatening and objectionable. Because all forms of growth are slow and gradual, we must face boredom, impatience, self-doubt, and even fear if we are to move to deeper levels of who we are.

One of our greatest fears in life is that of extinction. This fear can be so great that it compels us to resort to frantic attempts to "save our lives." We commit ourselves to establishing a strong, secure, and comprehensible "self" that can withstand the unpredictable and mysterious forces in our environment. This compulsion to survive at all costs and on our terms shuts us off from the good news that we have already been saved. We do not need to establish or create ourselves. God has already implanted a deeper and more real self in the depths of our hearts. We have already embarked upon a journey to liberate this real self in the company of God. Everything that happens to us can be turned into liberating influences and growth-producing events. But these things cost a little bit more. They challenge us to greater faith, hope, and patient love.

Another great fear we must face is that of the unknown. Our introduction into self-awareness may have been unduly influenced by a mechanistic understanding of the human condition. Such an understanding tends to oversimplify our growth processes and shut out experience that does not support a simplistic understanding of ourselves. When we embark upon a journey of authentic growth, these abandoned areas must be reclaimed and integrated into our total identity. Unfortunately, these same areas may have been regarded as enemies or dangerous to our psychological welfare. At the very least, they were regarded as strangers or unknown factors in our lives. Now, on the old road, we are going to meet them and face the fear of listening to their story of alienation and oppression.

We have touched briefly on some of the fears that have to be faced on the old road. But many more positive experiences await us. We have already learned that traveling on this road reveals the true story of our life. This will receive much more attention in the next chapter. We have also learned that this old road will teach us how to slow down and be reflective, to listen to God telling us our story in our hearts. Listening to this story will teach us wisdom and will enable us to see the road on which God wants us to travel. Finally, at the end of this back road we will discover a house. This is the home God intends for us, our real home. It possesses the secret of who we really are. When we arrive at its front steps, a deeper stage of our journey will begin. God waits at the door to accompany us on this venture of recovery and restoration.

But we do not need to wait till we reach the front steps of our house in order to experience a sense of new hope in our lives. Once we commit ourselves to a journey on the old road, things will begin to happen. After the initial fears of unfamiliar places and people have subsided, a deeper sense of peace will gradually arise from somewhere deep within us. The nature and source of this inner peace is not easily described. It will have something to do with an expectation of arriving at a long-awaited destination or the inner sense of security at discovering that we are now on the way that leads to home. An indefinable sense of relief that we are now in touch, however tentatively, with our inner core will arise in us. We are now coming home after many years of exile.

People and events will begin to speak to us in a new way. Most of these new insights will have to do with our past. A strong message will emerge concerning unfinished business left over from our earliest years. Memories from our past may come crowding back asking to be addressed. We are not to be afraid. These memories are simply all the rich elements of our story seeking to be heard, redeemed, refined, and integrated into the story of our journey so far.

One rich source of our early story will be found in our dreams. This is a wholesome service designed by God to ensure that we are aware of his healing presence on our journey. It works something like this. During our waking, conscious moments we are not always able to process the many experiences that cross our paths. At night our dream life tries to resolve the tensions from the day and defuse any threats in our daily experience. We dream even if we cannot recall our dreams. If we do not consider our dream life to be significant, then the energy needed to remember our dreams is not released. Only when we signal to the unconscious manager of our energies that we wish to recall dreams will we remember them.

Our dream life is not confined to resolving unfinished business from our daily experiences. Its services extend to our past experiences as well. If we have cut ourselves off from deeper levels of our being and have left dynamic issues in our unconscious unattended, then our dream life may try to connect with the root of these issues and resolve the unfinished business. Dreams that try to address this type of tension are usually thematic. They recur regularly and usually have a central theme. Sometimes these dreams cause fear — we call them nightmares. But they are easily recognized because of the recurring theme. Such a dream may indicate some outstanding issue in our life that needs our urgent attention.

I would like to share with you an example from my own life. I only began to appreciate the meaning of this dream once I became aware of the unfinished business from my past. This dream or nightmare involves a frightening experience, but once I tried to listen to it and learn its hidden wisdom, the area of neglect became quite clear.

In my dream I am a little boy once more. I awake in the middle of the night, still in the dream. There are no sounds in the house. I wonder where everybody has disappeared to. I wander around the deserted house in terror. I can find no one. It suddenly dawns on me — I am alone in the house. Everyone has gone away. I am now abandoned in this strange house and no one can hear my cries. At this stage I usually wake up in great fear.

With the help of a very caring and trustworthy mentor I was able to interpret this recurring dream. For most of my early adult life I was busy trying to establish a significant role that would also provide a significant identity. I was over-invested in the new road and in a quest for a home of my own making instead of the house God had provided for me. My real home had become deserted and even hostile. But now there was an urgent appeal from deep within me to return to my real home and reclaim the abandoned boy within. Like the tourist at the beginning of the chapter, I met a child who invited me on a deep interior journey to reclaim my true home.

You might be familiar with this theme of the abandoned child. Many writers, both psychological and spiritual, refer to this topic.[13] St. Thérèse of Lisieux drew our attention to the recovery of this abandoned child and presented it as the bedrock of all spiritual growth and development. Poets saw its relevance for healing and authentic human growth. G.W. Russell (A.E.), in his poem "Germinal," has this to say:

> In ancient shadows and twilights
> Where childhood had strayed,
> The world's great sorrows were born
> And its heroes were made,
> In the lost boyhood of Judas
> Christ was betrayed.[14]

And Antoine de Saint Exupèry exquisitely captures the real drama of the human journey in *The Little Prince*. He offers us the stages of real spiritual growth in a world over-invested with power struggles and the acquisition of material wealth. The story goes like this. A very competent pilot was flying his airplane over North Africa one day when, to his dismay, he crashed somewhere in the Sahara desert. This pilot, a highly skilled mechanic, knew everything there was to know about machines. As the seriousness of the crash dawned on him, the horrible significance of the desert began to register also. Although he possessed only a wrench and a hammer, he set about trying to repair the engine. In despair he had to give up. As night approached he sank into a deep sleep. He was awakened from his slumbers by the persistent questioning of a small boy. The pilot had no idea where he had come from, so he called him his little prince.

I suggest the following interpretation. The pilot is a highly skilled mechanic — a very functional person. He is able to reach for the stars and rise above all the obstacles that slow down earth-bound creatures. While riding high one day, a crash lands him in a desert miles away from fast highways and bereft of any resources that might meet his functional demands. He is reduced to a state of helplessness. His pathetic tools are totally inadequate to deal with his crisis. What is he to do?

In the throes of our worst troubles, when exhaustion reaches its highest point, sleep is often the only escape. It is then that we are sometimes awakened by the anguish of our lost child looking for a parent, just as the abandoned little boy emerged from within the pilot. The pilot is forced to face up to the reality of who he is. He is now confronted with a new task, the challenge of recovering the abandoned boy whom he calls "The Little Prince." The pilot must now learn how to cultivate the way of the heart. The book is about the story of his journey. When both have learned to walk together and the pilot learns how to parent the boy, both find the well, hidden in the desert. This is the source of real life and the secret of the hidden self.

We can search the libraries of the world and consult the most distinguished experts but the real secret of Christian growth could still elude us. To be certain of finding it we must find our abandoned child. It is this child who will tell us what we must do. At least, this is what Jesus seems to say. In Matthew's gospel, he says: "I bless you, Father, Lord of heaven and of earth, for hiding these things from the learned and the clever and revealing them to mere children" (Mt 11:25). Later, he is even more specific.

> At this time the disciples came to Jesus and said, "Who is the greatest in the kingdom of heaven?" So he called a little child to him and set the child in front of them. Then he said, "I tell you solemnly, unless you change and become like little children you will never enter the kingdom of heaven. And so, the one who makes himself as little as this little child is the greatest in the kingdom of heaven" (Mt 18:1–4).

Here we have a most revealing insight into the kingdom Jesus came to establish. It is founded on the original plan of God, who wishes to restore the true humanity of his people by teaching them to find the entrance to the way of the heart.

Once we become involved with God's original and unique plan for each one of us, the life story of Jesus may take on a more dynamic meaning. We may uncover an interesting insight into *his* journey of growth if we reflect on an incident from his early life (Lk 2:41–52). Jesus is like us in all things but sin, which means that he had to undergo a human growth process. Thankfully, Jesus grew up in an enlightened home under the wise love of Mary and Joseph. As a healthy boy, at the age of twelve he was anxious to find his real self and launch

himself along the fast highway in life. An exciting opportunity presented itself to him: When he was with his
parents and friends in Jerusalem he would slip away
and head for the Temple, the center of significant activity. While he was there, the brilliance of his intellect was
admired. He was now well and truly launched on the
way of the head.

The boy Jesus temporarily forgot that he had caring
parents. They on their part searched for him for three
days, all over Jerusalem. At last they found him, in the
midst of the head people of that time, the doctors of
the law. When his parents demanded to know how he
could do such a thing to them, he was so engrossed in
his intellectual activities that he could not understand
why they were looking for him. He said, "Did you not
know that I must be busy with my Father's affairs?"
The gospel is discreetly silent on the argument that must
have followed, but we do know that Jesus, like many
adolescents before him and since, lost the argument. The
next scene is one of subdued compliance as he follows
his parents to his real home where a lot of unfinished
growth business awaits him. It is then that the gospel
tells us that Jesus increased in wisdom, in stature, and
in favor with his heavenly Father and with other people.

This incident, which is often glossed over by spiritual writers, can offer us some fruitful reflections. Jesus
is anxious to become immersed in functional activities,
what we might call his role in life. He is tired of the slow
back alleys of his childhood and the lessons about his
real self that must be learned. He thinks that he knows
who he is and who he wants to be. He wants to do
something worthwhile. This same interior dialogue goes
on inside each one of us. Sadly, the dialogue may not
last very long. We may be hastily pushed onto the fast
highways by our parents and others who claim to know

what is best for us. In Jesus' case, the betrayal of his true self was temporary, lasting only until the intervention of good parenting brought him back to the authentic path of growth and development. In our case, the betrayal can last much longer. If we are lucky, at some stage of our adulthood we will be forced off the main roads of our life and invited on a journey of recovery. But once we arrive at the front steps of our house, we may well ask, "How do we become caring parents to this abandoned child within us?" To answer this question in any meaningful way, we need to reflect on an outline of Christian growth and development. This outline can help us understand the work that needs to be done.

The first significant dimension of our being — the child dimension — takes shape in the very early stages of our journey. Here we form our first significant impressions of ourselves and of life in general. Because we live in a highly functional world, most cultures use childhood to prepare for adult responsibility. This is as it should be. We cannot remain children all our lives. This becomes a danger, however, when a society abuses childhood in a frantic effort to ensure that the young person becomes a hyperfunctional adult. This can happen in two different ways. In poor societies where the struggle for existence is more intense, parents can become so ambitious for their children that every waking moment of the child's life is an intense preparation for a worthwhile career. In more affluent circles, children are allowed to rush too quickly into the privileges of an adult world. The end result in either case is that the child experiences a hasty and insensitive passage through this very significant childhood phase and leaves behind a lot of unfinished business. In fact sometimes we can leave behind a very battered child in our mad scramble for adulthood.

This early child stage of our development represents a historical phase of our journey. It is important to remember that this stage also represents a contemporary level of our being. We do not abandon this childhood stage forever, discarding it like a used container. If we attempt to do this, much to our surprise, we discover it years later, battered and neglected, waiting to be restored as the core of our being. This child part of us contains the actual and potential gifts and talents that await further development in a later stage of growth. It contains the limitations that circumscribe and define our gifts and talents. This child stage of development represents the world of emotions and feelings, our primary means of communication with the outside world before we developed our intellectual capacities. It contains the rich world of the unconscious and early significant memories. It is the source of our vulnerability and fragility. It also contains God's original dream for creation, which Jesus calls the kingdom. The child within us has the special gifts of this kingdom: poetry, artistry, prophecy, mysticism, and play.[15] These gifts will only be recovered if the battered child within us has been healed and restored.

The second important level of our being is the adult dimension. This grows out of our childhood phase or dimension through a process of *maturation*. This dimension begins to take over once our intellectual and volitional powers arrive at a certain stage of development. It envelops the child stage as the fruit envelops the life-giving kernel or seed. At this stage we begin to take control of our lives and are capable of making competent decisions. It is the center of learning and decision making, and the center of our defense and coping systems. This adult dimension is the center of our control, our managerial or functional capacity. In the world's estimation, this is the stage we have all been waiting for and is considered to be our final psychological destination. All our life must be spent in perfecting this stage in order to become aggressive and successful competitors in the intensive swirl of adult functional affairs. Once we begin to lose our functional energy and competitive sharpness, then we become an embarrassment and are quietly moved aside into retirement.

If, as happens with many people, we remain trapped in an exaggerated form of this adult dimension, then our whole identity will be stunted. In the initial phases of our adult development a certain exaggeration is permitted. A temporary obsession with freedom, control, competency and a successful role in life is even healthy and something to be encouraged. Around our role and sense of competency we build our own identity. This sense of self, however, is supposed to be only a temporary identity and it is sometimes called our false or idealized identity.[16] Instead of being well grounded in our reality, it is built more on our wishful thinking or unrealistic ideals. The healthy ideal is that as we move through life and a variety of sobering experiences, we would gradually discard this temporary identity and begin to allow our deeper and truer identity to emerge. This would then introduce us to a richer dimension of our being. But this stage of development is often left undeveloped and I call it the good parent dimension. This final stage of our spiritual and human development grows out of and is an extension of the adult dimension. Many of us lack this dimension, which in turn contributes to most of our spiritual problems. We are called by God to develop our capacity for self-parenting.

The good parent dimension is the third vital element in our development. It generates what we have termed the true self. It comes into existence because of the liberation, healing, and recovery of the child dimension. Once we begin to develop this stage, we are on our way to recovering our full story and our true identity. We might describe its development very simply as the personification of the way of the heart. It is the combination of all the qualities involved in fostering life. It grows out of and is a further extension of the adult, or second, stage of growth, but is much more refined, sensitized, and Christianized. It can be developed only if two factors are present in our life: 1) an appropriate withdrawal from an over-involvement in the way of the head (reflective living); and 2) the recovery of our child dimension, which forces the adult dimension to learn self-parenting and to love like Christ.

Only when we learn how to love ourselves in this Christ-like fashion can we authentically love others. How can we expect God to reach out to others from our hearts if we have not yet found our hearts? How can we permit God to offer hospitality in our house, if it is mostly abandoned and closed?

We started this chapter by emphasizing the importance of being faithful to the road that eventually leads to our true home. The little boy in our opening story wisely stated that the length of each road is designed to get us to our desired destination. If we refuse to follow the full length then we jeopardize the very purpose of our journey. A tourist had walked from the railway station, which was situated about two miles outside the town. He was angry and demanded of a local boy why the station was built so far from the town. The boy simply replied, "So that it would be nearer to the trains."

Reflection Exercises

1. Before concentrating on going deeper into your life, review once more the preparations you have made for this interior journey: Have you grown in your appreciation of wisdom, reflective living, self-acceptance, and the way of the heart?

2. Try to imagine your style of being present to yourself in terms of living in a house. How would you describe this house?

3. Do you feel that your house is closed to God and to other people? Are you conscious of any locked rooms in your house?

4. Are you afraid to explore your house in the company of Jesus? If you have fears, try to identify them and talk them over with God and/or your mentor.

5. Can you identify any experiences in your life that might be associated with the child dimension of your being?

8

The Child's Story

A little boy got separated from his mother in a busy supermarket. He was in great distress and asked a passing shopper, "Did you, by any chance, see a woman with dark hair with a missing boy exactly like me?"

Many people today are so anxious to get ahead in the world that they leave their child behind, abandoned in a hectic world. Yet this significant dimension of our being possesses secrets of inestimable value. It holds the keys to our true home, as well as the earliest and most revealing chapters of our story. Many of our present styles of behavior, attitudes, and feelings have their beginnings in this early stage of our journey. In order to have a compassionate understanding of our struggles and difficulties, as well as the nurturing gentleness to address the roots of our problems, we must listen to this child within. This is how our interior journey begins.

Much of the attention of our parents or significant people may have been directed toward the adult they wanted us to become rather than to the child who was struggling then and there to become accepted. Therefore our present level of growth and development could be impoverished by a lack of being listened to and welcomed into the world of the child. This can create a condition of spiritual and psychological poverty that plagues our adult efforts to feel at home in our world.

In order to reflect on our style of being present to ourselves, to other people, and to our world, let us return once again to the image of a house.

From my early childhood I can recall how some houses seemed full of life and warmth, while others appeared to be deserted and closed to the world. One house in particular conveyed an air of sadness and reserve. It was inhabited by a widow and her only son. It was bigger than most of the houses in the village and was set back from the main street and the hurly-burly of village life. Our only contact with this lonely boy was sharing the same desk in school. His mother came each day to the school and shepherded him home, ensuring that he was not contaminated by our unruly behavior. The other children and I often stood outside the front gates of his house and vainly tried to contact him. Once we saw him briefly at one of the many front windows in the house, but it appeared that he was quickly pulled back into the oppressive anonymity of the sad house.

Looking at the guarded presence of some people toward the world, one cannot help thinking that somewhere within them a bewildered and lonely child is being shut away from access to our world. How many of us can really become present to other people and to their world? Do we not tend, like the sad house in my village, to stand apart from others as we desperately try to invest our functional conversations with a feigned concern. It is a sad reflection on our level of growth and development to learn that loneliness and interpersonal conflict are still very much with us despite our ability to turn our world into a global village. To begin to address this vexing problem of interpersonal communication, we must first address the more pressing problem of recovering the heart of our lives, the abandoned child within, and learning how to befriend and heal this graced source of warmth and vitality.

Another house in my village created an unforgettable impression for a completely different reason. In this case it was because of the joy and life that spilled out of this house and drew the whole street into its bosom. In this house, a child was allowed to be a child without creating chaos or unpleasant disturbances. Both parents could combine an easy tolerance with a firm hand. The door of this house was usually open and we children were heartily welcomed. An atmosphere of spontaneity and celebration prevailed despite the modesty of its financial support. This family had managed to turn their house into a center of life and hospitality for the whole village.

This is how I imagine a mature Christian to be present to our world: someone who lives in their house fully, and can open the heart of their home to the stranger seeking shelter and affirmation. This is how I imagine Jesus living in his house. The secret is very simple. In our Father's house, there are many rooms. Jesus has already taken up residence in these rooms and now waits for us to return to our true home and occupy it fully. He also wants us to heal and liberate the abandoned child in this house, so that the child's joy and spontaneity may turn it into a true home. It now remains for us to turn our attention to this abandoned child and consider what needs to be done to achieve healing and liberation.

By listening to the story of our child dimension we may discover two very important insights. First, we are still being unconsciously influenced in our adult behaviors by psychological structures left over from a childhood in which the child dimension of our being became submerged beneath an over-functional adult dimension. This child dimension was not extinguised. On the contrary, it continues to struggle desperately to survive, but in a distorted and disguised manner. If we wish to change our adult attitudes, behaviors, and feelings effectively, we must first explore the many possible ways our child dimension could be oppressed and distorted. This exploration could reveal the real source of our adult struggles.

The second insight might reveal to us how a particular oppression or distortion took place. Once we know the story behind the distortion, then the healing qualities required to deal with the distortion are usually generated. So let us now explore some possible areas of unfinished business that could still be contaminating the adult version of our story.

When we were children we did not always have direct access to reality. Some significant "other" intervened and interpreted reality for us. This was necessary since we are not impersonal machines but are immersed in a complex subjectivity. There was a real need for someone more experienced in the ways of the world to break down this complicated phenomenon of reality and present it to us in simplified segments. Significant people in our early life implanted in us certain shapes to ensure that we perceived reality and the world in a safe and predetermined fashion. This shaping of our perception resulted in what we might call perceptual models, structural shapes lodged in our head that put order and meaning into the confusion of reality rushing at us.

In their early forms, perceptual models are extremely simplistic. Moreover, they are not purely intellectual but have a very strong emotive component as well. The early enforcers and shapers of these models tended to associate them with goodness and badness, as well as with our personal identity. Our whole sense of security becomes tied up with our fidelity to these perceptual structures. To illustrate this last point, let me share an experience from my childhood.

When my sister was born there was great excitement in my home. But it also gave my mother a lot of work especially when it came to feeding my little sister. Various bottles and other implements had to be carefully sterilized and mixtures of baby food made up. It was always obvious when it was baby's "feeding time."

A house near us was occupied by a large and disorganized family. This family also had a new baby. But this family was lower down the social scale and did not subscribe to all the perceptual models honored in our house. Therefore, we children were banned from entering that house. Needless to say, I did not always obey my parents and surreptitiously made excursions to this house to compare notes between my little sister's progress and that of the baby in this house. One day while I was there the baby began to cry. Someone suggested that it was hungry. To my utter amazement, their feeding procedure was breathtakingly simple. The young mother simply opened her blouse and gave her breast to the baby. In a flash I realized that my mother had managed to get the whole business wrong. I could not wait to get home and give her the good news.

When I explained to my mother how the feeding procedure should be conducted, my good news was not joyfully received. On the contrary, my poor mother nearly had a seizure. She was horrified and immediately accused me of visiting that house against her express orders. But her main wrath was directed against my perceptions. She claimed that I did not see such dreadful things and that someone in "that house" had encouraged me to lie. When I finally convinced her that I had accepted her version of events, she calmed down. The incident convinced me that an uncensored and casual approach to reality was extremely hazardous. You must always be conscious of the shape in which you perceive things. If the shape does not fit, then what is happening before you is not true.

I offer you this cautionary tale from my childhood to underline the intensity with which some of these shapes are implanted in us. Is it any wonder that many of us retain some very primitive biases right into adulthood? To make matters even worse, we allow our identity and sense of worth to be unconsciously tied in with these perceptual shapes. That is why it is sometimes extremely difficult to eliminate our prejudices and simplistic views of life. If this inner child dimension has not been healed and reassured, the insidious insecurity that results from this unfinished business drags us back into the grip of these very early perceptual models. We can recognize these primitive structures when we passionately defend our views in a very defensive and unreasonable manner. Such a response usually means that we are in the grip of something from a very early stage of our life.

Even Jesus ran into such crude perceptual models. In trying to change an established image of God, Jesus was accused of blasphemy. Today, we witness a similar reaction in our attempts to broaden people's horizons. The normal process of development involves a continual negotiation with reality in order to refine, enlarge, and substitute our perceptual models in keeping with a deeper understanding of life. We are expected to explore reality from a wider perspective than the very limited view of reality provided by childhood. But if we feel threatened, hurt, or misunderstood, there is the tendency to cancel this open approach and revert back to earlier shapes. To help ourselves or other people to move beyond this underdeveloped level, we must address the frightened child hiding within the locked room of a crude perceptual model. Only when this child dimension senses that it is being heard and gently reassured will it risk moving out into other rooms of the house. When the child is allowed to tell its story, it will graciously yield its frightened grip on our besieged adult.

In opening up the locked rooms of our much neglected child dimension, we could discover some dangerously distorted feelings in addition to the untrained perceptions. Even if our parents were genuinely loving and caring in our early lives, like many people of their time they may not have been very concerned about emotional training. If they were ambitious for us they might have pushed us hard. We then became very anxious to achieve in order to please our parents. Our big enemies were our limitations, weaknesses, and vulnerabilities, yet these are essential ingredients in the mix of life. Without fully realizing what we are doing, we could gradually develop a mixture of shame and guilt, reinforced by our parents' and teachers' impatience with our vulnerabilities. As adults, we have to face the consequences of this oppression of our childhood sensitivities. We may now be conscious of the self-hate that inundates our consciousness whenever we fail to be super people.

I remember witnessing an incident in which a child's limitations were treated most oppressively. A young mother was making her way home from a modest shopping expedition with her little girl. The mother looked harassed and tired as she impatiently pushed a stroller in which she had placed her few purchases. Clinging to the side of this stroller was the little girl, who was just about able to walk. The mother regularly shrieked at the little girl to hurry up and blamed her for making them late for her husband's lunch. The little girl was crying pitifully and continued to struggle to keep up with the fast pace of the mother. It was not difficult to guess what was going on inside this little girl. She considered herself to be a nuisance and the cause of all the trouble that her poor mother had to endure. Yet the only problem in the unfortunate situation was that her legs were little and weak. She was a child and could not match the giant strides of her mother.

We need to spend some time gently reflecting on the level of our tolerance toward what we consider to be negative factors in our lives. Are some of these so-called negative factors still a source of insidious shame and guilt? Are we still punishing the littleness within us that struggled so heroically to grapple with an enormous task? We need to listen to our inner world tell its tale of heroism and valiant struggles to overcome forbidding obstacles. Why shut away in a dark room this weak and vulnerable part of ourselves simply because we are sometimes incapable of making the gigantic strides demanded of an idealized or false self?

If we make progress in our attempts at reflective living and begin to establish a trusting relationship with our inner child, we may notice that experiences that involve angry or sexual feelings immediately evoke feelings of fear, guilt, or shame. What might be going on in the unconscious cellars of our oppressed childhood?

Many adults do not realize the power of children's feelings. Children are exposed to what might be termed primal experiences, early, unavoidable experiences that are inextricably bound up with our human condition. We are all capable of naming them: joy, compassion, sorrow, fear, anger, guilt, loneliness, loss, sexuality, wonder, and so on. However, some of these primal experiences may acquire an unpleasant association because of an insensitive introduction into them. Many of us had a very strict religious upbringing and an angelic performance could have been presumed and demanded of us. Whenever we showed the slightest sexual curiosity or the slightest signs of anger, we were quickly brought to heel by being plunged into feelings of shame, guilt, and fear. Instead of registering the feelings of sexuality or anger, we registered the feelings that became associated with them, usually the controlling feelings of shame, guilt, or fear. This control may have extended beyond childhood if we were later exposed to an authoritarian style of discipline in our adult formation. Sadly, many devout Christian people are emotionally crippled by an overexposure to these controlling emotions.

We need to treat ourselves compassionately whenever we are confronted by such feelings. There is a healthy form of shame, fear, or guilt that is freed from the unreasonable perceptions of a hurting child. It does not cripple us or unduly discourage us, but rather indicates a need for conversion in some aspect of our behavior. Whenever we feel severely inhibited from celebrating the sacrament of reconciliation or facing some area of past experience with our mentor, let us be gentle with ourselves and take some time off for a reflective exercise. Recall that unreasonable feelings of shame or guilt have roots in our early life. We need to go back to this early period through the story of our child. After allowing this story to be recounted many times, our hurting inner child may slowly trust the superior wisdom of our inner good parent. Greater inner security will be established in our relationship with God who expresses his love and forgiveness through our good parent.

Most of the people who come to me for counseling struggle with what they regarded as feelings out of control. Life was intolerable because they felt overpowered by guilt, fear, anger, sadness, or sexual feelings. Once an organic basis to these troublesome feelings was discounted, styles of early emotional control were explored. We usually discovered that little attempt was made to integrate certain significant primal experiences within healthy boundaries.

Our feelings acquire appropriate boundaries when emotional development takes place. One of the simplest ways to explain this process of emotional development is to reflect on the example of learning how to swim. If a child is kept far away from the water he will never learn to swim. Unless a child is allowed to get into feelings, he will never learn how to develop them. Feelings will always be a very threatening phenomenon and if by chance he is pushed into these frightening feelings in later life, panic will ensue.

If a child is allowed to spend all his time just splashing around in the shallow end he will not learn how to acquire the skill of swimming. In the same way, a child, who is allowed to ventilate his feelings without being challenged to submit to the laws of reality governing the situation, he will end up having difficulty exercising appropriate emotional control. But if a child is taught how to swim, then the water becomes his friend and this new skill enhances the quality of his life. The child discovers the boundaries of the relationship between himself and the water and by observing the discipline that keeps him within these boundaries, he moves skillfully through the water. Likewise, it is possible to learn how to swim in our feelings and relate to our world within the secure boundaries of a well-developed affectivity.

I once witnessed a wonderful example of good emotional training while on a visit to some friends. The eldest child, a boy of about five, had suffered a severe disappointment. A trip with his father had to be cancelled because of a sudden change in his father's business plans. So the little boy had to remain at home and suffer this experience of loss. The young mother had received no formal training in child psychology, but she had a fund of good wisdom. She made no attempt to disguise the reality of the situation. His father would not come back to fetch him. Neither did she try to move the boy out of the experience by a variety of distractions. But she did lend him the support of her stronger ego. At regular intervals she interrupted her work to go over and give him a hug and assure him of her support and understanding. I was invited to do the same.

Throughout this exercise of support I noticed that the mother guarded against two exaggerated reactions. She showed sensitive awareness of his tendency to withdraw into himself by including him in everything. He was still very much a part of the family even though he was not able to respond in his usual good humor. This avoided creating the impression that he was in exile simply because he was struggling with a painful experience. It also gave a clear message that there was a boundary or limit to his withdrawal from family life. The second exaggerated reaction took the form of angry outbursts on the part of the little boy. On two separate occasions the boy tried to act out his anger and despair. Once he shouted out that his father hated him and had left him behind on purpose. The second incident involved his younger sister, who came in for a very rough displacement of his anger. On both occasions the mother intervened very swiftly and in no uncertain terms laid down the boundaries within which he was allowed to mourn.

All the right elements were present in this situation to ensure a healthy integration of the feeling of loss. First, there was the permission to enter into the experience and feel with his feelings. Second, his mother helped him to identify the particular feeling — mourning over the loss of a trip with his father. Third, he was encouraged to stay with the feeling. Fourth, he was supported and loved while in the throes of the feeling. Fifth, the reality of the situation was clarified by the mother so that his perception would be accurate. Sixth, he was made to stay within appropriate boundaries while struggling to stay with and express this feeling.

These key elements are necessary in order to develop healthy boundaries around a feeling. The little ego of the boy was being helped to cope very constructively with the feeling of loss, integrating it into his world of feelings. He was being trained to mourn in the manner originally designed by God. This same approach is necessary for all our feelings. A proper emotional training exercise is necessary at all stages of our growth because most of us, at some time or other, will need to finish some unfinished emotional training of our early years.

Certain feelings in our early childhood may have received such a severe condemnation that they were unconsciously banished to the cellars of our house. Usually such condemnation is reserved for anger and sexual feelings. To illustrate the process of repression, let us take the feeling of anger as an example.

Because of a parent's intolerance of any sign of anger on our part, we may have learned at an early age to swallow our anger. Our fear of retribution can be so great that we learn to switch off our capacity to register anger and appear to have no anger in our system. The anger is present but unconscious. Only the capacity to register it consciously has been switched off. This is repression. However, feelings are not discarded that easily. Two very serious consequences could develop. One, we build up a reservoir of repressed anger and have a big "slush fund" of this anger looking for any opportunity to get out.[17] Later we find ourselves becoming angry at the slightest provocation and earn ourselves the reputation of being short-tempered. Or we might discover that in certain situations we tend to "blow our top," with embarrassing results. The repressed anger is simply looking for an opportunity to be expressed and it is unconsciously being displaced on to convenient targets. Unfinished business from our past catches up with us.

Another very serious consequence of this unhealthy repression is the disguised and indirect expression of anger. This type of behavior is particularly frustrating because of the inability to recognize that anger is even involved. One indirect expression of anger can be manifested in physical symptoms of certain illnesses. If anger is switched on in the system, even though it is not consciously registered, it triggers the normal physiological responses that accompany all anger: raised blood pressure, increased heart rate, pupils dilated, an increase in various hormonal secretions, and many more such responses. If the anger is not dealt with and cleared from the system, then these physiological responses continue until chronic, psychosomatic symptoms develop. We might have problems sleeping, bouts of depression, or pervasive feelings of shame or acute anxiety, due to anger bottled up in our system. Only our physician can make such a diagnosis, but more and more medical practitioners are becoming convinced that our psychological condition determines much of our physical well-being. Our anger and its healthy development can play a vital part in our spiritual and physical health.

For release of repressed feelings, outside help is necessary. We need someone to help us recognize our disguised and indirect expressions of feelings. We need someone to enable us to express these feelings directly. We also need a safe environment in which to work off our backlog of repressed anger. Many people find that a group situation designed to explore feelings provides such an accepting environment. If sharing and reflecting on our life with a trusted mentor does not address these problems, we may have to seek out the help of a trained counselor or psychotherapist. But we should do what we can within the limits of our situation. The main thrust of healing in this area will take the form of shedding light into the dark and neglected corners of our deserted house in order to uncover repressed areas of our vulnerable humanity. Our prayers should lead us in this direction in any spiritual attempt at healing.

In this chapter we have reviewed elements of unfinished business that we could find in the child dimension of our being. We have briefly seen how some of us can live like prisoners in our own houses, trapped by the distortions of this unfinished business. Our child dimension is begging us to return to this area of our life and try to understand what happened in the early stages of our journey. Such an understanding will give the abandoned child the freedom of our house and release our adult dimension from a crippling and mystifying bondage. Compassion and hope could flood back into our lives simply by listening to the story of our child.

What may have become very clear from our review of this early stage of childhood is the absence of a responsible parenting dimension in our being. The following story might indicate that it is more prevalent than we might realize.

A little boy got separated from his mother in a very large and busy department store. Since this frequently happened to him, he kept calm. He made his way to the lost-and-found office and asked the lady on duty, "Have any missing parents been handed in recently?"

Reflection Exercises

1. Reflecting on your experience, do you sense that influences at work in your present life have roots in your early childhood?

2. Try to identify a concrete example of a prejudice or an over-simplified view left over from your early training. Examine this perceptual model for a few minutes. Now, without sacrificing some important value, see how you can extend the range of your understanding or compassion toward the people or the situation.

3. Are you aware of excessive feelings of shame or guilt in your life? Do you think those feelings come from the objective gravity of certain misdemeanors? Or do they come from some mysterious influence dating from your childhood? Make the decision to tackle a particular set of these feelings.

4. Which feelings do you find most difficult to handle? How do you react when confronted with these feelings?

— Become depressed and self-condemnatory?

— Give in to the feelings and act them out?

— Seek out some distraction by which to avoid the feeling?

In the future, try to apply some of the principles involved in emotional development that you may have learned in this chapter.

5. Have you encountered situations in which certain feelings should have been invoked in you but, instead,

you felt nothing? If you are aware of such experiences, discuss them with a trusted friend or counselor in order to assess the degree of possible repression.

6. Ask God for the grace to experience his spirit of truth in your feelings.

9

The Adult's Story

A tourist and a local man were sharing a railway carriage on a rail journey. The tourist had just finished reading all the newspapers and magazines he had brought to kill the journey. Only then did he take an interest in his companion on the other side of the carriage. To his horror, he noticed that his fellow passenger appeared to be in great distress. He was staring intently out the window, his head moving from side to side while he seemed to be gasping out numbers. The tourist, thinking that he might be having a stroke, asked him if he was feeling alright.

The local inhabitant replied impatiently, "You have distracted me and now I have lost count!"

"I am sorry," said the tourist, "but I did not understand what was happening to you."

"Well, I will tell you," said the local passenger. "I make this journey quite often and I find it long and monotonous. So I have arranged a little project for myself in order to pass the time. I count all the sheep between my departure point and my destination."

"But that is an impossible task," exclaimed the tourist. "You mean to tell me that you count all the sheep in each field as we go past?!"

"It is not impossible," replied the passenger. "The trick is this: First you count the legs of the sheep and then you just divide by four!"

This introductory story caricatures principal features of a conventional understanding of the adult stage of growth and development, sometimes called the ego dimension. At this stage it is presumed that we have the freedom and maturity to decide on a destination and to be capable of organizing a journey to get there! We also assume that we have the resourcefulness to defend ourselves against unpleasant experiences such as boredom. Undoubtedly we have considerable potential to learn new ways of coping with a variety of challenging situations. In short, we are admirably equipped to excel at the way of the head or the functional approach to life. Sadly, we may also have developed to a sophisticated degree the capacity to waste valuable energy in childish escape mechanisms. We too could be engaged in counting the legs of sheep in order to distract us from experiences that do not seem to contribute to our external accomplishments. If we listen to our adult's story, we realize how much of our energy is devoted to this limited expression of adulthood and why we allow our abandoned child to languish in obscurity. This becomes possible if we kill the journey toward real growth and spiritual development by confining ourselves to the logical roads of the false self.

As we improve in our ability to reflect we may begin to discern our personal style of relating to ourselves and to the world. Soon we realize that something within us does not ring true, as if, having tried very hard to become the type of person everybody wanted us to become, we now feel betrayed and misled. We may have sacrificed many interests and pleasures to attain what we considered to be a worthwhile role, yet inside we feel hollow and unauthentic. Gradually it begins to dawn on us that we have been working from a false base. Our present identity and self-image are "ready-made." They have little to do with our past history, deeper feelings, and real interests. In short, we could be living out of a false idea of who we really are.

When we enter into life many of us, thankfully, enter into a caring family and community. All our needs are lovingly supplied and the significant people in our life wish us the best. One need that is eagerly supplied is our need to know *who we are.* At every moment of our existence we have people who do not hesitate to help us define ourselves. Obviously, not all the elements of this definition are true. Some may be too negative, but they are offered in the hope that they will spur us on to greater efforts. Other elements are too positive and can give us an inflated sense of who we are. But regardless we need to know who people think we are because we have not yet developed the capacity to figure out our identity for ourselves.

Sadly, this reliance on other people's estimation can do serious harm to our self-esteem. Some cultures do not believe in praising their children. They think this will ensure that the child is submissive and dependent. A religious or moral dimension operating in these cultures may very well add a connotation of being bad and sinful. At some point all of us find that we have to define ourselves by something tangible, something over which we have some control. Most often this stage occurs during adolescence and young adulthood, when our role in life provides us with new incentives and opportunities to realize who we are. For a while we may believe that we have found our real selves by selecting a role that gives us some sense of significance and value. As we grow, in deeper self-knowledge and general maturity, however, we are also meant to recover more of the person beneath the role. In other words, we are supposed to embark upon a second journey, an interior journey, by which we return to the heart of who we are and find the key to our real identity, the real self.

This brief description of the origins of our sense of identity is obviously simplified, but it may be sufficient to alert us to one further vital task in the area of self-definition — the gradual erosion of the false self. In order to launch us in life, significant people, for good or for ill, helped us to assemble a convenient, ready-made identity. This was intended to be temporary until we became established in life. Unfortunately, many of us do not realize this and we spend our adult energies trying desperately to vindicate to ourselves and to the world this contrived idea of who we are. This sense of who we are is primarily functional and therefore limited. Once we take control of our lives, and have finished the early adult tasks of role definition, we are supposed to deepen our self-awareness and self-knowledge. This will enhance our appreciation of our identity and help us to move toward uncovering the real self. It means uncovering our real story and dismantling the convenient cover story that is no longer necessary. Sadly, not everyone recognizes the need for this process. Some of us manage to resist all attempts to uncover our real self until our unhappiness becomes so acute that we are forced to face what is really going on in our lives. We sometimes manage to kill those elements of our journey that might invite us into a truer sense of self by our own ingenious version of "leg counting." This ability to resist the truth is accomplished by what psychologists call our defense mechanisms. The unhealthy use of such stratagems enables us to maintain our false cover story. To understand how our adult dimension might be resisting God's call to deeper growth, let us look at some of these defense mechanisms.

Due to our highly functional educational formation, we may display a defense mechanism known as intellectualization. This is the capacity to extract the intellectual components from an experience and discard the emotional elements. In situations in which the rational dimension is considered to be paramount, the intellectualizing process will be encouraged. For instance if I have the unfortunate experience of being mugged and relieved of my wallet, the police will be interested only in the bare rational bones of the experience. They will encourage me to discard the emotional components and stick to the facts. In other words, they will encourage me to intellectualize the experience. It will be left to sympathetic friends or a counselor to help me relive and come to terms with, the full emotional experience.

This adult capacity enables us to resist the call of the child within or, once having answered that call, to rob the child's story of its true significance. Our child dimension mainly communicates through feelings, as we have seen. Unless we listen to the real story beneath the feelings, the wisdom offered by the child will be missed. Intellectualization can never go that deep since it is primarily invested in removing ideas from the messy context of the emotions.

A more common defense mechanism is rationalization, which involves ignoring the real reason for our actions and substituting a more reasonable sounding one. This process can take place consciously or unconsciously. For instance, on being told by friends that we seem to be a bit depressed, we immediately assure them that we've simply been working very hard recently and that a few days rest will put everything to rights. In fact the real reason why we are depressed may be due to some unfinished business from our childhood demanding attention.

When the fictitious reason is a religious one, we move into the area of spiritualization. This defense is commonly applied by fervently religious people and usually involves attributing directly to God or the devil something that has its roots closer to home. For example some people might find it more acceptable to believe that sexual desires are planted in them by the devil rather than to acknowledge that such desires come from a healthy expression of their own human condition.

From this brief description of rationalization and spiritualization, we can easily see how God can be resisted in our experience. The real source of our story can be easily dismissed and replaced by a more acceptable and reasonable sounding explanation.

One defense mechanism common to us all is denial. It tries to give a questionable security to the child in all of us. Again it may work at a conscious or unconscious level. It is a very early defense mechanism and is frequently observed in children. The child can conveniently ignore elements in his or her environment that are inconvenient. For example, he or she leaves a mess and when called upon to account for it, expresses bafflement as to how it got there. As adults, we too have the uncanny knack of ignoring elements in our experience that are inconvenient at certain times. We might forget certain appointments because we might have to face some threatening experience. Such a defense mechanism is also at work in communities in which severe social problems are mysteriously ignored. A person who later becomes conscious of these problems is at a loss to know how this social blindness was possible. Obviously our adult dimension can easily resort to this childish mechanism when God challenges us on our journey to listen to some vital bit of wisdom. When people exclaim that they are totally baffled as to how they could have allowed so many years to go by without realizing that something was going on in their lives, they probably made convenient use of denial.

Another convenient defense mechanism is regression. It must be immediately explained that there is a healthy form of regression. Most of us when we play, relax, or share deeply with a good friend or mentor regress to an earlier level of our being. This is a healing exercise consciously adopted in the service of our authentic well-being. However, we have to be aware of the unhealthy form regression can take. An old saying, "If we cannot beat them, let us join them," applies here. If we are under pressure from the troubled child within us, there is the real temptation to adopt an unhealthy tactic of appeasement. Instead of the adult dimension adopting a responsible attitude to the demands of this child, there is capitulation. We become childish and give in to the childish demands. This could be expressed in over-indulgence in alcohol or food. It might also be expressed in extreme behaviors of hopelessness or powerlessness. Unless we are seriously ill, whether physically or mentally, we must be very careful about acting out our feelings of being powerless. Our adult dimension has been richly endowed by God with spiritual and psychological resources that are the incarnational channels of God's strength within us, which we sometimes recognize as "grace." But such resources need to be continually activated by prayer and by wise and courageous decisions.

In the last chapter, we encountered a defense mechanism known as repression. When feelings become so threatening that we are unable to cope with them consciously, we have the capacity to unconsciously push them into the cellar. But this tactic provides very inadequate protection. While locked up in the cellars of our house, our repressed feelings can take on sinister proportions. Repression can be a healthy defense tactic if it offers temporary relief from an intensely painful experience, but it must never be adopted over the long term in order to avoid back roads of our journey or threatening rooms in our house.

Two more fairly common defenses could be operative in our attempts to escape from authentic Christian growth. One is hyperactivity. If we suffer from low self-esteem then we try, unconsciously and sometimes consciously, to compensate by an over-investment in external achievements. The sad consequence of this type of compensatory behavior is that it does not work. In fact, the harder we work to compensate for this lack of esteem, the more our hunger for approval increases, or our feelings of failure intensify. We can become intensely compulsive about our accomplishments. This dynamic often leads beyond overwork to burnout.

Another common defense is an emotional remoteness. This is often seen in celibate lifestyles, in which people may be capable of casual friendships but in reality are afraid of real intimacy. This attitude is an extension of the repression of feelings and alienates us from the tender core of the child dimension. When we are out of touch with this inner core, it tends to become an area of threat in our lives. If someone enters our life who wishes to get close to us, then we are unwittingly forced to face up to this dimension. If the threat is too great, we move away from it by keeping the person at an emotional distance. This emotional isolation results in an insidious loneliness that increases our sense of worthlessness. To allow someone to get to know us, we have to get to know ourselves at the deepest level and to recognize that our defensive tactics are locking up vital aspects of our selves.

One very common defense mechanism requires our special attention, since it may be at the root of much cruelty, hatred, oppression, and maybe even war itself. This is the defense tactic called projection. It works something like this. If I unconsciously dislike certain feelings or desires within me then I attempt to disown them by projecting them outward on to someone else. These feelings and desires often belong to our abandoned child dimension and do not fit in neatly with our idealized or false self. Therefore, we could be tempted to get rid of them in this irresponsible manner. The sad result is that we only "observe the splinter in your brother's eye and never notice the plank in your own" (Lk 6:41). In other words, we see the unacceptable side of ourselves only in others and seek to punish them for it instead of owning it in ourselves.

A short poem by Erich Fromm admirably sums up what our journey to the heart tries to accomplish. It also places this pervasive tendency toward projection in a universal context and thereby alerts us to its potential dangers:

> Only by "knowing the heart of the stranger"
> do I see behind the social screen
> that masks me from myself as a human being,
> do I know myself as the "universal man."
> Once I have discovered the stranger within myself,
> I cannot hate the stranger outside of myself,
> because he has ceased to be a stranger to me.
> The command "love thy enemy" is implied already

in the Old Testament command:
"love the stranger."
If the stranger is the stranger within me,
the enemy is also the enemy within me;
he ceases to be the enemy, because he is I.[18]

We have been concentrating on some very complex processes involved in our struggle to grow toward the real self. We must be careful lest we give an impression that stopping the unhealthy use of these defense mechanisms is an easy matter. From a very early age these attempts to escape from the truth in our lives operate. All we have read so far about the difficulty we have accepting our real self and the powerful seduction of the idealized or false self is at work in our addiction to these stratagems. We need the help of God's redeeming grace as well as all the encouragement of those precious people sent into our lives by God to help us on our journey. Above all, we need to capture the excitement in our story that emerges when we withdraw from the false roads of our journey and face the redemptive back roads. We need to reflect on the beauty and integrity of the real self once it is rescued from beneath the defensive layers of our false self. For this reason, a story might not be out of place. It vividly illustrates our struggle with the false self and the strength of our resistance to God's invitation to reveal our true selves.

One time a friend of mine who was a builder intended to renovate a very old house. This building had acquired many kinds of extensions and modifications over the centuries. He wanted to remain faithful to the original design, but he was unable to identify the early part of the building. So he brought in an expert who requested to be left alone with the house for a few days. This expert wanted the house to tell its story and reveal its secrets. After some time he contacted the builder and told him the good news: he had uncovered the original design of the house.

Before the builder would lay a hammer on this build-ing to clear away the false walls and additions, he had to uncover for himself the true and original design. In a similar manner our true self may be obscured by an unhealthy use of defense mechanisms. God is the expert on our interior journey, telling us the true story of our house. Our adult dimension possesses the restorative capacity of the builder but this same dimension needs to spend some time learning how to be a restorer after God's own heart. To uncover the real self, we must lis-ten to the story of the abandoned child as well as to the story of the adult's misguided attempts to erect a self superior to God's original design.

Even though emphasis has been placed on the need for healing and restoring the abandoned child to a life-giving presence in our house, this does not mean a downgrading of the need for a strong ego or adult di-mension. A person can only accomplish this restorative work by acquiring an appropriately developed adult di-mension. This fact could be forgotten in certain forma-tion or therapy programs in which too much emphasis is placed on merely ventilating feelings. The result of such unenlightened formation could be an inability to estab-lish boundaries around fundamental experiences. Let us recall the story of the little boy whose mother helped him cope with an experience of loss. She was gentle and compassionate, but also strong. The goal of emotional development is endurance and courage. Anyone who has learned to negotiate the back roads of life and face the restoration of a house is tough in the best possible way. All journeys of any length and complexity involve stages of boredom that challenge our capacity for en-durance. To develop our ego or adult dimension further, we must face and even welcome such experiences. We will touch upon this concept again when we deal with the good parent dimension.

Another area of concern connected with the adult dimension has to do with the way of the head, or the functional approach to life. Because of the particular aim of this book, it might appear that the way of the head has been unfairly dismissed. It is worth repeating here that the way of the head is vitally important when required by a particular context. The problem with the way of the head arises when it becomes absolutized, or when it is adopted in contexts that require a different approach. Our obligation to grow and develop primarily requires the way of the heart, but this does not mean that the way of the head has no place in our repertoire of personal gifts. On the contrary, there are times when God demands that we be highly functional and efficient.

This caution is offered here because of a reaction by some people to their conversion from hyperfunctionalism. Our new-found enthusiasm for growth and self-development can generate an unbalanced irritation with anything to do with functionalism, which can be equally irresponsible. Essential tasks and services for ourselves and for others require a high degree of functional efficiency. We must continue to develop our adult dimension further, finding new and more efficient ways of organizing. When used in their proper contexts, they become God-given gifts for the work of promoting the reign of God.

We have just issued a caution on the need to be constantly alert to new ways of doing things, as well as the need to train our adult dimension to face up to new challenges. The mature and responsible person knows how to cope intelligently, efficiently, and appropriately with a given situation. This wisdom may not be confined to the human species but may also extend to the animal world.

Once upon a time an inexperienced hunter went out alone to hunt lions in a jungle. After some time he came upon a lion sitting in a clearing. Both saw each other at the same time. The hunter prepared to fire his gun and the lion prepared to spring upon the hunter. The hunter fired but missed the lion. Before he could reload, the lion sprang but leaped too far. It sailed over the hunter's head into some very thick undergrowth. The hunter had time to beat a hasty retreat and escape.

Later, back at the hunting lodge, he regaled his fellow hunters with this incredible story of a narrow escape. The guide who was in charge of the expedition was not amused. He told the hunter that he had better make sure that he never missed a lion again at such close range. He ordered him out to practice his shooting. As the hunter was practicing he occasionally heard a heavy thudding sound. After a while he decided to investigate the source of the sound. He came to a clearing and saw an amazing sight: the same lion — practicing its leaps!

Reflection Exercises

1. Are you conscious of hiding behind a mask in your dealings with others? Do you find it difficult to reveal yourself to people you consider to be friends?

2. Do you invest most of your self-esteem in your achievements and in your role performance?

3. Have you developed a healthy adult dimension? Do you find it relatively easy to organize your life? Or

do you need to acquire more will power and managerial ability?

4. Review the defense mechanisms once more. Try to identify the mechanism (or mechanisms) through which you tend to escape from growth opportunities.

5. Try to imagine how Jesus exercised his adult dimension.

10

The Unhelpful Traveling Companion

A little boy was traveling on his own in an over-crowded bus. He had a head cold and occasionally sniffed rather loudly. A haughty and severe looking lady tourist sitting beside him could contain her irritation no longer. "Have you got such a thing as a handkerchief?" she snapped. "I have," said the little boy, "but I don't lend it to strangers!"

Not all people who accompany us on our journey have our good at heart. Part of growing into the wisdom of the journey is being able to recognize who is really for us. We are going to meet people, hear stories, receive directions, but which are authentic and in step with God? One traveling companion in particular must be identified and exposed: the tyrannical and underdeveloped area within us that tries to control our lives and rob us of a healthy personal autonomy. We briefly touched on this in chapter eight. This undeveloped part of our psychological make-up can easily intimidate us, discourage us, make us feel excessively guilty, and seriously hamper our journey of healing and restoration. I call this element within us "the bad parent."

If we find that we avoid many back roads of our journey because of a fearful and distrustful attitude to the unknown and unfamiliar, then we could still be in the grip of this tyrannical element within. Again, if we discover that we have shut up many rooms in our house and that we are trying to eke out a joyless existence in a cramped front room, this bad parent could be in possession of our home. This mysterious and sinister force in our lives casts a shadow of disapproval on many of our normal experiences and on many of the decisions we make on our own. Morally underdeveloped people often mistakenly identify this as "conscience." It is also mistakenly regarded as the sensible presence of "God," with sad consequences for the practice of religion. This bad parent tells a most untruthful and unfair version of our story. This can dishearten us on our journey and alienate us from our true home. So let us first explore how this intimidating force came into being.

Like many things in our lives, the bad parent started out serving a necessary and useful purpose but was allowed to overstay its welcome. Its function begins very early in life. As little children we did not have the capacity to be self-directing and morally autonomous. We needed the psychological support, guidance, and protection of our parents. We continually checked with a significant parental figure to see if we were in good favor. If we felt accepted and approved of, then we felt good and worthwhile. But if we felt out of favor, then we felt rejected and frightened. Through no real fault of our parents, our early sense of acceptance could easily develop into a conditional form: pleasing our parents. The sad result of this development could be too great a reliance on the approval of parental figures, including God, in gauging our level of self-worth. We end up with a tyrannical parent inside us, harshly judging us and blindly controlling our lives. Let me give a simplified explanation of how such a condemnatory parent develops within us.

Take a typical scene from a child's early life. The child, sitting within easy reach of mother, is playing with a teddy bear. While the child is nice and loving toward teddy, mother is pleased and communicates a strong signal of approval. After a while the child becomes bored and decides to investigate the inside of the toy bear by trying to pull the head off. Mother sees this murderous act and is horrified. She must put a stop to this behavior immediately and attempt to eradicate the roots of such destructive tendencies. She imprints on the child's imagination a powerful impression of being naughty. The nice and approving parent turns into a punitive parent and the child feels bad and rejected. The impression of this punitive parent remains inside the child. This is a primitive control mechanism but we must remember that the child is still very underdeveloped. The parent wants the impression to last, and so she regularly reinforces it when her child acts out of character.

A few days later the child is playing in the backyard when the cat comes out. The child is away from mother's controlling presence. The child strokes the cat with affection until he becomes curious about what makes the cat work. As he reaches for the cat's head he stops. Something inside him makes him register fear. He expects a punitive parent to descend upon him. The cat gets a reprieve because the punitive parent inside the child is now in operation. So the child begins to behave himself in his parents' absence because the primitive control mechanism is serving its purpose.

Unfortunately some parents overdo the programming and the child registers this punitive parent too intensely. Serious emotional damage can be inflicted. In my capacity as a counselor I have met many people who have struggled intensely with a powerful "bad parent." In some the intense early programming was followed by a repressive adult formation and as a result very little emotional autonomy was allowed to develop.

We have to be careful when using the term "bad parent" that we do not give the impression that any parent who tries to control his or her children is bad. This primitive control mechanism can only be termed "bad" if it inhibits the moral and spiritual growth of the child. As already indicated, this severe parenting process is intended to be only a very temporary measure of control while the child is incapable of a more sophisticated response. As the child develops its tiny adult capacities of reflection, discrimination, and decision, it is ready to be introduced into another form of discipline. At this more advanced stage the child should be offered an explanation of the morality of the situation, a description of the values involved, and an opportunity to select the desired value. In other words the child is given an opportunity to "own" his decision to be good. This might be described as internalization.

Sadly, this more sophisticated and refined control system is not always allowed to develop adequately in people who come from strongly authoritarian backgrounds. The unrelenting power exercised by authority figures in some homes and cultures could produce a distorted person. An extreme example of this control might be found in the following incident.

I was traveling down some back roads in a remote part of Ireland one time and became hopelessly lost. The fact that it was night only made matters worse. I stopped at a house that was in darkness and I presumed that the people were in bed. In desperation I knocked on the door hoping someone might hear me. After a little while a window opened overhead and a fairly elderly lady demanded to know what I wanted. I explained my predicament. She said that I was to wait there and she would send down the boy. Naturally, I expected at least an adolescent to appear. The gentleman who eventually appeared was at least in his early sixties. He gave me directions and we talked for a while. He was unmarried and it was his mother who had addressed me from the window. From our conversation it was not difficult to construct his psychological situation. He was an obedient son who would not dare question the authoritarian role exercised by his mother. It can be presumed that other authoritarian influences at work in his life were also left unchallenged.

In subtle and not so subtle ways people can be ushered along a path laid down for them by their moral betters. This might seem to be a safe way by which to instill such important Christian virtues as obedience and respect for God's laws. In reality it promotes a level of religious response more in keeping with very young children. For many religious people obedience consists of learning how to placate a very non-Christian image of God. This approach to obedience in reality promotes an unhealthy alliance with the "bad parent" element of themselves. This collusion sets up a train of connections with primitive elements in the immature human condition. The unredeemed child element is reinforced, the false self is supported, and an insidious anger is generated.

When all these elements operate unconsciously, it becomes obvious that the expression of Christianity that results offers little inspiration to the younger generation or to a deeply reflective group of people who are repelled by some forms of organized Christian religion. We end up with an expression of Christianity that views the world in totalitarian terms, is insensitive to the oppression going on in the world, as well as being spiritually narcissistic and humanly repressive. All this takes place because of a lack of awareness of how essential it is to ensure that as a person grows spiritually, he or she must also grow humanly. So let us take a closer look at what can happen when this profound truth is ignored.

We can see that the primary purpose of the bad parent is to maintain control. We can also appreciate how this primitive psychic structure can be unwittingly cultivated by religious authorities who understand obedience as unquestioning compliance. This restricted understanding of obedience fails to address the need for a more adult response to God's will. This same limited understanding of obedience, with its primary emphasis on control, could lend itself unconsciously to an unhealthy collusion with the bad parent dimension of our being. In fact, such an unconscious collusion with the bad parent could discredit the most fundamental form of Christ-like obedience.

To better understand this, we need to look at two possible types of obedience. In an earlier chapter, we made an important distinction between two approaches in life: the way of the head, required in highly functional situations, and the way of the heart, required in growth oriented situations. This gives rise to two different types of obedience. A conventional understanding of obedience tends to involve functional or institutional obedience. While important, this type of obedience must be confined to its appropriate context: critical situations that demand efficiency and coordination under a central authority, for example, obedience to an army general in a war situation, to a captain in charge of a fire brigade, to a surgeon in charge of a complicated operation, or to a religious authority involved with a serious but complex moral issue. But such functional situations do not exhaust all the possibilities in our daily experience. Other elements of who we are require a more personal and searching response. Growing in our human experience and in God's presence in our lives cannot be reduced to the clear-cut instructions of a functional authority. To reduce all forms of obedience to this level would trap people in a stunted state of development. People who remain in the grip of the "bad parent" often welcome and even glorify this functional type of obedience.

Radical Christ-like obedience transcends these necessary but functional situations. This form of obedience belongs more to the growth approach to life or to the way of the heart. It involves finding our personal and special path in life. The story of our journey is the history of our obedient response to the radical command of God to grow and become the person he has called us to be. People capable of this type of obedience do not become trapped in unhealthy subjectivism or lose contact with the community and church in which they live. On the contrary, people who find their own hearts, relate to the hearts of others and of the church. But some religious circles still experience great unease about this more personal type of obedience. Yet this is how we internalize Christian values, how God's law comes to be written on our hearts and not on tablets of stone.

"Owning our house" is a figurative way of describing the process of internalizing values with which most of us are familiar. This approach to cultivating God's plan for us is more in keeping with our dignity as adult persons, appealing to many, even most, of our human and spiritual capacities. This approach aims to generate within us that necessary wisdom that enables us to identify the roads of our life's journey. Once having embarked upon our journey and discovered our true home, this same wisdom enables us to uncover the real design of our house. It is simply an application of the way of the heart. The authoritarian approach appeals to the way of the head and is more invested in external conformity to public signposts and prescribed highways than in mysterious journeys.

To reconcile a person to his journey and motivate him to restore his house (which is what internalization involves), the way of the heart requires the following approach. First, a relationship of trust, respect, patience, and support is essential between the guide and the person striving to cultivate the value. This supportive relationship empowers the person to face up to the intimidating fear caused by the "bad parent." For a while, until we reduce the bad parent element to a manageable size, we will feel insecure and guilty when we try to identify a value on our own. Therefore, we need all the support and understanding we can muster from authority figures while this exorcism of the bad parent is taking place.

Second, sufficient space and time is necessary for the person to develop a readiness to assess the value and eventually choose it as his or her own. Reclaiming a house is a slow and delicate business. Cultivating confidence in the discerning powers of our wisdom is also a slow and complex exercise. Extricating ourselves from the authoritarian style of the bad parent is a slow growth process and its laws must be respected.

Third, we need to recognize that feeling lost or undergoing a crisis of confidence in institutional authority is just a temporary experience which, in reality, is a graced stage toward internalization. In order to cultivate our inner direction-finding capacities, we must be prepared to get lost on the way. In like manner, to develop our own discerning qualities we must spend the required time trying to work out the puzzling design of our house.

Fourth, allowances must be made for a temporary resistance to the value until the feelings and varied perspectives have been explored. In all growth exercises, there is a period of struggle before the right path is adopted. At first, when we uncover the real story of our house and begin to assess its condition, there is sometimes a temporary rebellion against the situation. Various strategies are explored before there is, finally, a gracious acceptance that this is the only house that can provide us with a true home.

The outcome of taking full responsibility for our lives is an inner-directed and truly loving person whose response to God's plan comes from the heart. Taking on this responsibility and acquiring an inner sense of Christ-like goodness could be interpreted as an unhealthy individualism or a disregard for legitimate authority. Nothing could be further from the truth. Finding God deep within ourselves, and learning to love his healing ways opens us to his healing movements in other people and especially to the movement of his Spirit restoring the church. The spirit that now pervades our house is, according to Christ, one of wisdom and friendship. "I shall not call you servants any more, because a servant does not know his master's business; I call you friends, because I have made known to you everything I have learnt from my Father" (Jn 15:15).

A sign that we are growing and facing up to our bad parent is the measure of our capacity to stand up for the truth and sustain the disapproval of certain people on our journey. It means that we are growing in personal autonomy and mature responsibility. The following story illustrates this kind of self-assurance.

A tourist was exploring some back roads in a remote corner in Ireland. He came to a crossroads with no signposts. He wanted to get back into the local village.

Rather than risk getting hopelessly lost, he decided to remain in his automobile and wait for a local inhabitant to arrive. After a considerable length of time a local man arrived on a bicycle. The tourist greeted him warmly and said, "Well, Paddy, am I glad to see you. I want to know which of these roads will take me back into the village." "How did you know that my name is Paddy?" asked the local man. "Oh, I just guessed it," replied the tourist. "Well, in that case, you can guess which is the right road!" said the local man as he rode angrily away.

Reflection Exercises

1. Do you have difficulty with authority figures? Do you adopt a very docile attitude toward them? Or do you adopt an aggressive attitude toward them? If you uncover an area of difficulty, discuss it with your mentor in order to determine how distressing this issue is for you.

2. Do you think that you have a problem with the issue of control in your life? Do you find it difficult to allow other people their space when it might affect you? Do you find it easy to trust people's ability to make good decisions?

3. To what extent are you trying to cultivate greater moral and religious autonomy? Are you trying to internalize religious and moral values or do you allow religious authority to decide everything for you?

4. How would you evaluate your relationship with God? Is this relationship trustful and open? Is there still a shadow of the punitive parent in this relationship?

11

Cultivating the Good Parent

A small boy wanting to cross a busy street was waiting anxiously for a break in the traffic. A lady tourist who seemed to be lost was also anxiously looking across the street. The little boy, remembering his manners and how he must be kind to tourists, plucked up his courage and said gallantly, "May I help you across the street, Ma'am?"

"Oh, no thank you," said the tourist. "You are very kind, but I can manage on my own."

"Well, in that case," said the little boy quietly, "would you mind helping me across?"[19]

We have arrived at the third dimension of our being. I call this the good parent dimension. We have met this dimension already in previous chapters but here we will explore it in more depth and bring the various strands together. This level of development results from the adult's recovery and healing of the abandoned child within. When we decide to change our ways, we begin to cultivate this nurturing dimension of our being. Since it grows out of our adult dimension, it begins to develop as soon as we cease being totally preoccupied with our functional tasks and begin devoting some of our adult energies to our growth tasks.

Once we embark upon a journey of growth and healing, each dimension of our being serves and supports the other. This is the moral of our opening story. The little boy is secure enough to reach out and offer to help the perplexed tourist. The tourist is secure enough to manage this functional task on her own. Then the little boy recognizes his limitations and invites the tourist into a parenting role. The recovery and care of the child dimension converts the adult dimension from an obsession with external achievements to the nurturing role of healing and restoration; the adult dimension realizes that a child dimension has been abandoned and mounts the rescue operation. From this restorative effort on the part of the adult the parent dimension emerges. And so the creative interchange between the different levels continues. This complementary interdependence among the three dimensions uncovers the real self. Once this growth approach has been applied to our lives, we become nurturing and authentically loving toward others. Authentic and Christian growth is never for oneself alone. It is primarily intended for service of the reign of God and the realization of God's dream.

Once we decide to take responsibility for our journey and begin the restoration of our house, the nurturing qualities required of a good parent become obvious. These parental qualities or virtues can easily be identified. Here we will review some of them — acceptance, kindness, openness to truth, listening, patience, compassion, firmness, and respect for our uniqueness as individuals.

We have established in an earlier chapter that *acceptance* is the best starting place for our journey. Here we will explore it in the context of parenting. Of all the qualities required by a good parent, this is probably the

most important. Superficial gestures of tolerance are totally inadequate for building self-love in the child. What
matters is the *acceptance of the reality of the child.* If a parent does not really accept a child, then all the material
comforts in the world will not compensate for this radical rejection. Sometimes parents think that they have
accepted the reality of the child when in fact they have
accepted an idealized version of their own making. In
such a situation, the real child is punished for not living
up to this unrealistic notion of childhood.

In a similar manner we could deal with the child
dimension of our own lives. In a sentimental moment
we might take pride in a superficial child-like attitude.
When confronted with the needs and responsibilities of
the real child within, however, we may not want to own
responsibility for it. That is why we must frequently re-
new our reconciliation with and acceptance of this mysterious element of our being. A most sacred moment for
this profound act of acceptance is in the holy eucharist.
Christ does not hesitate to become fully present under
the humble species of ordinary bread and wine. Likewise, by this act that repeats the yes of our redemption,
we are invited to allow Christ to become fully present
in us under the real species of our humanity.

Kindness is basically the same as acceptance of our human reality. This word comes from the concept "kind,"
which means nature, sort, or species. To be kind is
to allow someone to be fully the nature originally designed by God; to be unkind is to regard someone as
being less than who they really are. Jesus is kindness
personified because he came among us and accepted
us as we truly are and did not make us feel inferior
or ashamed of our human condition. To regard ourselves as being either superhuman or inferior to

others is a most unkind and therefore unchristian attitude. In some people's early lives, a lack of kindness on the part of early significant people reinforced a tendency to construct a compensatory false self. There is nothing so unkind to us and our real possibilities as this false self.

We encountered *openness to truth* in an earlier chapter when reviewing the importance of reflective living. Truth reveals the full plan of God's love for us. Through this means God will try to reveal our true selves. At every moment of our existence God offers us this good news. Sadly, we often cultivate such an artificial identity that the liberating truth of God finds it hard to break through. Nevertheless, truth tries unceasingly to remove the concealing coat of paint that hides the real grain of the true self. Apart from insights into hitherto unknown personality characteristics, such as being introverted or tough-minded, this liberating truth will also enlighten us as to the unique style of our defense mechanisms or even such behavior patterns as disguised expressions of anger. Whatever the insight, and no matter how painful, it will always offer us genuine directions for our journey of growth.

We must bear in mind, however, that the process of removing defensive walls is usually painful. Because it is part of the human condition to feel a little raw and exposed after some new insight into our behavior, the restorative work of God must always be carried out with great gentleness. We must always be mindful of the tender core of our being. The image of a child proves helpful here because it generates in us the sensitivity of a good parent dealing with a vulnerable child. The good parent is gentle but he or she is also truthful in keeping with the child's readiness to receive the truth. Good parents always respect the truth of the child because they respect the truth in themselves.

Respect for the truth is the real test of authentic friendship. The providential stranger on our journey has a special gift for us. It takes the form of some particular insight or element of our story that opens us up to the real purpose of our journey. If we possess openness to truth, as well as gentleness in applying it, then the stranger feels empowered to share his or her gift with us. If we are closed to truth, no matter how religious we claim to be, we deny the presence of God in the stranger sent to walk with us on our journey. We will never recognize God on our journey to Emmaus.

From my own personal experience I have discovered that even good friends find it difficult to convey challenging but liberating truths. When I recommend this in conferences or lectures, I am invariably told how a seemingly good friendship ended because of a well-intentioned attempt to pass on some helpful insight. Yet, if we reflect for a moment, we will realize how loving such an attempt really is. Can you imagine a good friend of yours allowing you to walk around without knowing that you have some comical label pinned on your back? It is much the same with our behavior patterns or styles of relating to our environment. We can have a blind spot concerning our impact on people that can have detrimental consequences for our spiritual and social welfare.

Listening means being able to sit quietly with ourselves in an accepting and receptive mood until we slowly learn to recognize the unique pattern of our heart's movements. Again, as we have seen in an earlier chapter, it is a vital element of reflective living. Just like any art or skill, the ability to listen is cultivated by dedicated practice.

Some of us might find this kind of listening to be a challenging exercise. We should try to set aside a quiet period toward the end of the day when we can try to listen to what is going on in our world of feelings. For a while we may only register surface impressions from our more immediate consciousness. All kinds of projects, plans, and ideas might invade our consciousness. But after some time we will begin to move deeper into the stream of our consciousness and recognize and read our moods. A whole range of feelings can be unconsciously registered as we move through our daily routine. Many of these feelings have roots in our childhood experiences. Some of these seemingly fragmented feelings also form a thematic pattern. For instance, it is possible to go for months and even years in a job, in a way of life, or in a particular group of so-called friends without realizing how unhappy you are in such situations. Only when you thread the fragmented feelings together in a reflective exercise can you discern the prevailing mood. God can use this same process to attract us to a particular way of life or to undertake some creative project. But, again, we can allow God to go unheeded and unheard because we do not take the time to allow the feelings to emerge and to identify the distinctive and providential pattern.

Feelings appropriately registered and refined by reflective living are often more reliable than the intellect in discerning the laws of wisdom and the paths God wants us to travel. Such a reflective approach to both our daily and our past experiences is truly listening with the heart. Once we begin to cultivate this nurturing quality toward our own hearts, then we also begin to cultivate the art of listening to the heart of the other person. Such Christ-like presence to another person is sometimes called listening with the "third ear." The greatest gift that we can give to another is the gift of their own real heart, but it can only be uncovered by our own liberated and healed heart.

A priest friend of mine shared an amusing experience that involved cultivating the art of listening. So taken was he with the subject that he devised a retreat for boys that involved an awareness walk in the countryside. One day he brought the boys into a field, asked them to sit quietly for a while and then try to record mentally all the sounds of which they were aware. When it came time to share what sounds they had heard, he was amazed that every boy claimed to have heard mechanical sounds. Only then did he himself become aware of distant traffic on a highway. He had been inundated with the sounds one would normally expect in the country: birds singing, bees buzzing, and so on. But what really amazed the entire group was their failure to register the sound they most needed to hear — the shouts of an irate farmer desperately trying to get them out of the field because an equally irate bull was in the vicinity! Authentic listening involves hearing what is *really* there and not just hearing what one expects to be there or hopes is there.

Some people confuse *patience* with passivity, but there is a world of difference between them. Passivity is simply non-action compounded by a failure to respond in a responsible manner to a situation. Superficially, patience might seem to be non-action, but in fact there is always an adequate and appropriate response. Patience presupposes that the action required by the situation has been taken. Now it is only a matter of waiting for events to take their course. For instance, patience is exercised by the gardener who has properly prepared the soil, sowed the seeds, and must now wait for the growth process to unfold. Mere passivity on the gardener's part would allow the garden to run wild.

On the human level, patience is exercised when a growth approach, or the way of the heart, has been adopted. The appropriate response to the situation has been made; now nothing remains to be done except wait for the outcome. When we first attempt to cultivate patience, it may seem to be a fruitless exercise. But once we become familiar with this type of response to a situation, we will be amazed at how wise and kind this attitude to life can be. This response protects both body and soul from the ravages of aggression; it can also soothe and calm the nervous reactions of our inner child.

Compassion means "to suffer with." It is often used as another word for pity, but a useful distinction can be made between them. Some people fear that the challenge of cultivating a healthy self-love promotes self-pity instead, and we all know that self-pity is a debilitating quality. Pity on its own is merely a feeling of empathy with or sympathy for someone in a painful situation, but pity does not always move a person to help someone in distress.

We might look to the gospel story of the good Samaritan to see an illustration of the difference between pity and genuine compassion. Many people passed the unfortunate victim lying wounded on the side of the road. They had pity for him but they passed by. The good Samaritan arrived and opened himself to compassion. First he saw the victim and registered pity. Pity, the first element of compassion, enables us to feel what it is like to be in a distressing situation. However, he did not let it rest there. He got down off his donkey and moved toward the person suffering. This is the second key element in compassion. We are with the person in pain. Pity on its own keeps us at a distance. Third, he was not afraid to inflict redemptive pain on the person in distress. He loved the person so much that he was able to overcome the victim's resistance to being moved and transported him to an inn, a more suitable place of healing. These three elements of compassion go beyond mere pity.

We all need a compassionate understanding and acceptance of our struggles and the world of our inner child. But we must guard against merely feeling sorry for ourselves. Self-pity robs us of our self-respect and of access to God's regenerative grace. Compassion for ourselves moves us to adopt the caring and healing action that activates God's grace. Our good parent dimension has compassion for the child within, which enables us to cultivate a healthy self-compassion. This is not a passive and defeatist quality. Rather, self-compassion is restorative and healing. It promotes mercy and forgiveness for being human and vulnerable. It eliminates the corrosive experience of alienation and self-rejection that can plague us for years. Finally, self-compassion enables us to face up to the redemptive pain of self-discipline and the need at times to make hard decisions for our authentic well-being.

Yet another nurturing quality of the good parent is *firmness*. This is not merely a mechanism of self-control, but rather a *healthy self-discipline*. We emphasize the importance of a compassionate self-discipline for growth and development. The child within needs firm boundaries in which to negotiate increasingly complex experiences. The adult dimension also needs healthy boundaries in order to respond creatively to life's challenges. Therefore compassionate firmness is most necessary to ensure that our growth is solidly grounded on God's law of reality and love.

Respect for our uniqueness as individuals is an essential element of our good parent dimension. When God created us, his incredible creativity ensured that each person would be governed by an original plan. Because this uniqueness is an integral part of our being, any attempt to foster our growth must respect this phenomenon. All good parents recognize this precious dimension in their children: we, too, must safeguard this divine richness within. Uniqueness and originality enhance God's creation and generate a dynamic variety within the human family. This healthy originality must not be confused with an unhealthy singularity and egocentricity that reduces harmony. We need to develop the ability to appropriately choose our particular road and at the same time draw on the wisdom of the stranger.

We have reviewed in this chapter only some of the qualities that promote human and spiritual growth. This list of qualities was never intended to be exhaustive. It provides us with examples of the parental or nurturing qualities that constitute the healing relationship of self-parenting. These qualities also constitute the chief characteristics of the way of the heart, or the growth approach to life. The good parent dimension emerges from this sensitive and creative combination of nurturing qualities.

We could have mentioned the vital quality of wisdom — insights gained from a profound self-knowledge and from the actual art of parenting. We could also have said a lot about justice. Justice involves maintaining God's right order in our relationships with ourselves, with others, and, of course, with God. We have to begin by making sure that we recognize and honor that right relationship with ourselves. The quality of this relationship determines the quality of our relationships with others. Justice of the heart is the foundation of all our concerns for justice.

We could also have expanded further the quality of endurance or fidelity that parents must have in their love for their children. Good parents do not give up easily on their children despite the trials and pain a growth process involves. Neither does God give up on us because of our failures and struggles. Therefore, we must never give up on ourselves. We must always be faithful to the road opening up before us and be prepared to endure whatever it takes to complete our journey of growth and development.

One of the most important fruits of the parenting process is self-transcendence. This healing service liberates us from unhealthy self-absorption. Just as healthy parenting of a child frees him from hyperdependency and over-concern for his needs, the same liberating exercise can take place in us as a result of our self-parenting. We are now free to give ourselves to others in a more spontaneous and nonmanipulative manner. Because we are now growing in internal freedom and autonomy, we are able to offer this same freedom to others. We are especially able to let God be God in our life and in our service of others.

The good parent dimension is not developed once and for all. Rather, it is a growth process that will continue until the day we die. What really generates the good parent in the first place is the decision to begin the restorative process. Once we commit ourselves to recovering and healing the abandoned child, then the growth process begins. So it is not a question of how much of the road we have traveled. Rather it is a question of whether or not we are facing in the right direction. God, in creating us, put us on the right road. Some of us, however, might need to check whether we are going in the right direction. As we progressed through this book, we have simply spent some time together listening to our hearts and checking directions for our journey in life.

In developing the good parent dimension of our being, we allow God full movement in our lives. It is no coincidence that the parental qualities necessary for our complete healing and restoration correspond with the fruits of the Holy Spirit. In St. Paul's letter to the Galatians we read: "What the Spirit brings is very different: love, joy, peace, patience, kindness, goodness, trustfulness, gentleness and self-control" (Gal 5:22–23). And again in St. Paul's letter to the Corinthians we have a description of this love and of the way of the heart: "Love is always patient and kind; it is never jealous; love is never boastful or conceited; it is never rude or selfish; it does not take offense, and is not resentful. Love takes no pleasure in other people's sins but delights in the truth; it is always ready to excuse, to trust, to hope, and to endure whatever comes" (1 Cor 13:4–7).

We can make another connection which, though profound, is in no way presumptuous. We have been made in the image and likeness of God. As we grow and develop, we take on more and more of this likeness. Within the blessed trinity, three persons constitute the fullness of the godhead. Likewise in us, three dimensions or levels constitute our full being and real self. In the trinity, the Son proceeds from the Father through generation. From the love between the Father and the Son proceeds the Holy Spirit. In us the adult proceeds from the child through maturation. The love between the adult and the child produces the good parent. Between all levels of life, especially within life's original source, the blessed trinity, there is a mutual giving and receiving. Likewise in us, the flow of life is generated through the loving relationships between the various levels of being. This is how God's plan of love is realized in the growth process — it is simply a story of love generated on a journey in life.

Let us return and leave the last word to the special story that, for me, has shed much light on our journey together. It is a quotation from *The Little Prince* at a stage in the story where a truly nurturing relationship has been established between the boy and the pilot. The pilot has learned how to comfort and listen to the boy. The boy has transformed the pilot and taught him how to see with the eyes of the heart. They are now able to walk together in the desert in search of the well of clear water. The pilot, like any caring parent, is sensitive to the limitations of the child. In their journey together, the child gets tired but the pilot is able to carry this delightful burden. As he travels let us listen in on a parental reflection made by the pilot.

> As the little prince dropped off to sleep, I took him in my arms and set out walking once more. I felt deeply moved, and stirred. It seemed to me that I was carrying a very fragile treasure. It seemed to me, even, that there was nothing more fragile on all the Earth. In the moonlight I looked at his pale forehead, his closed eyes, his locks of hair that trembled in the wind, and I said to myself: "What I see here is nothing but a shell. What is most important is invisible . . ."
>
> As his lips opened slightly with the suspicion of a half-smile, I said to myself, again: "What moves me so deeply, about this little prince who is sleeping here, is his loyalty to a flower — the image of a rose that shines through his whole being like the flame of a lamp, even when he is asleep. . . ." And I felt him to be more fragile still. I felt the need of protecting him, as if he himself were a flame that might be extinguished by a little puff of wind. . . .
>
> And, as I walked on so, I found the well, at daybreak.[20]

Reflection Exercises

1. To what extent have you developed a healthy self-parenting capacity?

2. Review once again the parental qualities described in this chapter in order to see how you rate with each one.

3. In coping with your struggles, can you distinguish between self-pity and self-compassion?

4. Try to identify a parental quality not listed in this chapter and rate your performance in this area.

5. At regular intervals, for example, every two months, review your progress in self-parenting with your mentor or with God in prayer.

Part 3

In Search of Companions for the Journey...

12

Our Journey Together

Once upon a time a village had a very serious problem. It had no children. All the women were well beyond child-bearing age. There seemed to be little hope for the future of this community.

The village elders, who formed the governing council, met in an emergency session. They set up a working committee to travel the countryside searching for young people to settle in their village.

At last a young couple agreed to come and settle with them. To add to the elders' delight, the young wife was pregnant. The working party was responsible for overseeing the arrangements to make the young people feel at home. The young couple were shown the village and the house in which they were to live.

In order to ensure that the new life would be of the greatest benefit to the community, the working committee had drawn up a program covering every aspect of the child's life. When the young mother-to-be studied this program, she was appalled. She felt that she should have some say in the rearing of her child. She realized, too, that the program was more concerned with the maintenance of the community's prestige than with the unique development of her child.

The young woman challenged the wisdom of the council of elders. In an emergency session, the council decided that the young couple *must* submit to their wisdom, as they were responsible for everyone in the village without exception. The young couple decided to leave.

The council continued their search for new life, well pleased with their vigilance and strength of resolve. The young couple continued their search for a new home carrying with them the promise of new life.

This story vividly illustrates the difference between the way of the head and the way of the heart. In this final chapter we will look at the community dimension of our lives in the light of these two ways. Community here is used in a very general way to include small Christian communities, parishes, religious institutes, and the church on a diocesan, regional, and universal level.

When we journey together by the way of the head, we are part of an institution or an organization. Only when we travel together by the way of the heart can we talk about true community. The quality of a community is determined by its commitment to developing life in all its fullness. The quality of an institution is determined by its effectiveness in maintaining control and combatting the forces it was designed to overcome. Just as on an individual level we can confuse functional performance with growth, likewise at a communal level we can confuse institutional maintenance with community building.

As individuals we are called by God to go on a journey of growth and development. Likewise, a community is called into the same experience. Much of the pain I hear from people today has to do with their being trapped in over-institutionalized communities. Many of these people leave these "communities" in order to seek true soul companions. Many others remain functionally attached to their institutions but their hearts are seeking or have already made life-giving connections with strangers on the road.

The great temptation facing all communities is to ignore the back roads and confine all their energies to the fast highways. External results, legal conformity, efficiency in performance, material and spiritual security, status, and survival become the main objects of attention. Uncovering the real self of the community is ignored. The crises, the searching, and the drama of the real story of the journey are avoided. What remains is often a highly organized group of cautious people providing a soulless refuge from the promptings of God's Spirit. Meanwhile the strangers continue on their journey, moving ever closer in their search for the real story, carrying with them the hunger for a real community.

We spoke earlier about the growth process that gradually eliminates the false self in order to uncover the real self that contains the original and unique plan of the person God intends us to be. We also illustrated how this growth process can be usurped by a maintenance of the false self in the mistaken belief that life is best served by a rigid conformity to a functional way of living. This same process can also occur on a communal level. An institution may increase in size while striving primarily to maintain its status and power. It resists change as an enemy of stable identity and functional effectiveness. A real Christian community, on the other hand, obeys the law of spiritual growth laid down by Christ. It yields up its temporary identity (false self) in the service of new life and the call to uncover its deeper meaning (real self).

Just as we need a providential stranger on our road to alert us to our tendency to follow the way of the head and avoid the way of the heart, similarly on our journey *together* we need the loving service of providential strangers. To challenge the dominance of an institutionalism that stays with the way of the head, we need to be alerted to the manner in which too great a reliance on the institution oppresses life. Those who alert us to this danger in order to promote community are called prophets. These prophets are necessary in every Christian context that claims to be involved in community building.

Two forces are at work in any growth process. First, spontaneous flow of life strives to actualize the rich potential assigned to it by God. Second, life must be channelled through an order or structure in order to realize God's design. These two forces are at work in all growth processes and give rise to a creative tension that results in dynamic life. By maintaining a healthy balance in this conflict, growth is generated.

The prophet tries to alert us to an imbalance in the interaction between these two forces. Because we distrust the spontaneous flow of life, the imbalance is usually toward striving for too great a control. Because of this, institutional oppression is the customary object of the prophet's concern.

Whenever we try to contain and direct the life of a group or an individual by structures or rules an imbalance is likely to happen. In order to be secure and in control, people responsible for directing a group or community tend to exercise too much power. This usually results in oppressive structures that merely maintain order rather than foster life. Institutions or organizations usually have a functional task of dealing with some threat from the environment. Promoting the growth and development of its members is too often secondary to this primary goal. Even when it claims to be promoting life, it can unwittingly oppress life through outdated and unnecessary structures. The prophet alerts the institution to this oppression.

Every Christian group that strives to be an authentic community and to promote spiritual and human growth must have a healthy and creative tension between the two forces of life. This gives rise to the need for two types of leadership.

Official leadership tries to maintain control over the flow of life and regulate people's behavior in the service of public order or institutional discipline. Official leaders are selected and appointed by the institution or community. It may be a pope, bishop, parish pastor, religious superior, or some other institutional leader. We are all familiar with this type of leadership. For many people, it is the only possible kind.

A second type of leadership, which is not as well known, is called prophetic or charismatic leadership. Paradoxically, we find some of the finest examples of prophetic leadership today among the official leaders of religious institutes. This type of leadership complements the official role and tries to promote greater spontaneity in the flow of life. It challenges beliefs, structures, and practices that fail to do justice to new stirrings of growth. Prophetic leadership is not necessarily selected or appointed, since the Spirit breathes where it wills. However, since this same Spirit needs human mediators, we can offer ourselves for this service provided we have restored our own real self. Something will be said on this later.

Both kinds of leadership are necessary for fostering life within a community. Often they complement one another. Both must be exercised in a responsible manner. Since we are familiar with official or institutional leadership, we are also aware of most of the responsibilities associated with this role. We do not need to spend time on it apart from noting the serious responsibility of official leadership to acknowledge the complementary role of the prophet.

Prophetic leadership is most vulnerable to misunderstandings and resistance. Most of us will be uncomfortable with this type of leadership, particularly if we come from a highly institutionalized background where prophetic leadership was ridiculed and suppressed rather than encouraged. The tension it tries to create gives rise to an accusation that it is trying to undermine legitimate authority. In fact, the service offered by the prophet tries to save official leadership from being dictatorial and destructive. In short, it tries to move the living organism along its journey of growth and development to fulfill the purpose for which God called the community into existence. Prophetic leadership tries to liberate the community from a false and static understanding of self and to open it to the task of recovering its path to growth.

If we wish to love others in a Christ-like manner, then we must love ourselves as God originally intended us to love. This has been a constant theme running through this book. This involves a journey to the heart in order to unfold God's original plan for us imprinted on our hearts. To find our hearts we must uncover our vulnerable inner child. In healing this abandoned dimension, we begin to grow into the fullness of our being. We also develop the prophetic dimension of our lives.

By recovering the child dimension of our lives we cultivate that nurturing dimension called the good parent. Among the many qualities of this good parent is wisdom. This ability to see with the heart plays a most important part in prophetic discernment. An even deeper source of prophetic wisdom lies in the fact that the redeemed and healed child within offers us a special gift

implanted by God at the moment of creation — the secret of God's kingdom. This is a vision of what God's
reign will be like, a special access to the dream God
has for his people. This is the source of a peace and
joy the world cannot give, the way God wishes us to
journey together.

Before we embark upon a community building exercise certain conditions must be met. First, some attempt
must be made to initiate a personal growth program for
the individual members of the group. Unless the members in a community are in the process of individual
liberation and healing, the basic communal bond will be
flawed. From our reflections on the hidden and perni-
cious effects of resistance to growth and the unhealthy
use of defense mechanisms we can see how this flaw is
generated and how it operates. Many religious group-
ings are aware of the unhappiness that can be present
in a seemingly devout community that was deprived of
an authentic incarnational spiritual formation. Jesus may
have had this growth principle in mind when he warned
us about building a house on sand (see Mt 7:24–27).

Second, great care must be taken in selecting or in co-
operating with those who claim to be community build-
ers. Some people are genuinely innovative and, with the
best of intentions, are anxious to organize people. But if
these organizers have not traveled the way of the heart,
they are unable to resonate with the heart of the community. Their ideas are well suited for the functional
tasks confronting the community, but they lack the vision, sensitivity, wisdom, and other nurturing qualities
that can only come from many days spent on the journey
to the heart.

Third, the nurturing qualities necessary for individual growth and healing are also necessary in building or restoring a community. Within any community

(because it is a living organism) we can identify the three dynamic dimensions of child, adult, and good parent. An unchallenged adult within a community immediately turns the community into a coldly efficient organization. For a community to grow and to become healed, the battered child element within the community must be recovered and restored. In this way a community can recover the gift of play, of prayer, and of God's dream for the community. Through the exercise of nurturing the inner child, many beautiful things can happen to the community. Recall once more some of the good parent qualities and you will realize the way a truly Christian community relates to the world. Because the central quality in any parental relationship is the ability to listen and live reflectively, a Christian community of the heart must be a listening community. As a result of this openness to the Spirit of God speaking in the heart of each member, important messages for the church and for the world are received. This is how the prophetic dimension of a community is cultivated.

Fourth, great respect must be cultivated for the sacredness of each individual member. The sensitive environment in which the growth process must take place is a life-support system, exquisitely designed by God, in which the plan implanted in each heart unfolds. It is our unique way of entering into relationship with ourselves, with others, and with our world. We need to hear God speaking to us in many providential strangers and events, but these strangers must respect the unique twists and turns of our road and the personal style of our story. This *must* happen in a communal setting if the real richness of community growth is to take place. Strategies must be devised that allow the growth and development within the individual's heart to generate new and richer levels of relationship with others.

Today, despite the apparent breakdown in some social and religious structures, I believe something exciting is happening in people's hearts. The secret to the possibilities developing for community renewal lies in the deceptively simple challenge of Jesus to love our neighbors as ourselves. This command is beginning to take on new significance. We now know that any attempts at community building that ignore the basic hunger for a deeper expression of individual dignity and human growth will reap the prophetic anger of later ages. Nothing is sacred that impedes God's loving plan for his people, a plan of astonishing creativity and ecstatic hope. Each of us carries this tremendous dream of God in the depths of our hearts. Jesus has told us the secret of uncovering this dream. If we find the battered child within us and redeem it, this child will begin to dream.

Do not let structures, institutions, or the false prophets of doom inhibit you. Tell us your dreams bubbling up from the well of your liberated heart, because the world instinctively senses that something exciting is happening. We will share these dreams for the radical renewal of the church, of religious institutes, parishes, or any forum where people hunger to meet in a new way. Working together to realize these sacred dreams must be what Jesus meant by the reign of God.

It has been such a joy walking this short part of your journey with you. I thank you sincerely for allowing me to stay with you on this section of your road. I must also publicly express my gratitude for the precious gift given to me by those countless loving people who walked with me and shared their stories. The story I heard is your story because it is also my story. If we listen to it in the gentle quietness of our hearts, it will transform our journey together and reveal the dream of God. One last appeal: Do not underestimate the unique gift of your story and your journey. Please believe that in the depths of your heart a child possesses a priceless dream — the vision of the reign of God.

One more story before we go. A tourist had come to the end of his visit to Ireland. He was returning with the jarvey to a small village after his final tour of the countryside. It was evening and the sun was setting in the nearby hills. They had now become very good friends and were sad at the thought of parting. As they lingered a while before saying good-bye, they both watched the sunset. The tourist was moved to say, "This has to be the most beautiful sight in the world." And the jarvey modestly replied, "I suppose it is not a bad sunset for a village as small as ours."

Reflection Exercises

1. Spend a few minutes reviewing the various groups, societies, or communities of which you are a member. Try to identify those communities that still exercise an authoritarian style of leadership. Review strategies that might prudently allow you to call these groups to a more community-oriented leadership style.

2. How interested are you in exercising prophetic leadership? What movements or groups are you involved with that are striving to create a more hopeful world for the present as well as for the future? Do you have a dream for the world? What are you doing to realize this dream?

3. In dealing with your family, group, or parishioners, which type of leadership do you exercise or promote?

Do you subscribe to the principle that each person has special gifts to share with the community? Or are you primarily invested in conformity and control?

4. Seek out people or groups that share your dream in some way and review ways of working together.

Notes

1 See especially Diarmuid O'Murchu, M.S.C., *Coping With Change in the Modern World* (Cork: Mercier Press, 1987).

2 There are some excellent writings on the relationship between human growth and spiritual development. See, for example, the quarterly journal, *Human Development*, 400 Washington St., Hartford, CT 06106.

3 Eamon Kelly, *In My Father's Time* (Cork and Dublin: Mercier Press, 1978).

4 Claire M. Brissette, *Reflective Living* (Whitinsville, MA: Affirmation Books, 1983).

5 There is a considerable body of literature on stress and how to cope with it. In *Human Development*, Vol. One, No. 2, Summer 1980, an excellent article by James Gill, S.J., M.D. points out the connection between stress and physical illnesses.

6 The Institute of Creation Spirituality, P.O. Box 19216, Oakland, CA 94619, promotes this renewal of our relationship with our sacred environment.

7 Eamon Kelly, *Bless Me Father* (Cork and Dublin: Mercier Press, 1976).

8 Antoine de Saint Exupéry, *The Little Prince* (New York: A Harvest/HBJ Book, Harcourt Brace Jovanovich), p. 5.

9 Antoine de Saint Exupéry, p. 87.

10 Johannes B. Metz, *Poverty of Spirit* (New York/Mahwah, NJ: Paulist Press, 1968).

11 See the *Pastoral Constitution on the Church in the Modern World* (*Gaudium et Spes*), No. 22. *Vatican Council II: The Conciliar and Post Conciliar Documents*, ed. Austin Flannery, O.P. (New York: Costello Publishing, 1975).

12 Friedman, M. and Rosenmam, R., *Type A Behavior and Your Heart* (Greenwich, CT: Fawcett Paperback, 1974).

13 This theme of the neglected child within has been dealt with in various books and articles. I have found the following helpful:

Charles L. Whitfield, M.D., *Healing the Child Within* (Pompano Beach, FL: Health Communications, Inc., 1987).

W. Hugh Missildine, M.D., *Your Inner Child of the Past* (New York: Pocket Books, 1963).

Jane F. Becker, O.S.B., Ph.D., "Getting to Know Your Inner Child," *Human Development*, Vol. 10, No. 1, Spring 1989.

John Bradshaw, *Home Coming: Reclaiming and Championing Your Inner Child* (New York: Bantam Books, 1990).

14 "Germinal" by A.E., *The Faber Book of Irish Verse*, Edited by John Montague, (London and Boston: Faber and Faber, 1974), pp. 241–242.

15 See Noel Dermot O'Donoghue, O.D.C., "The Paradox of Prayer" in *Doctrine and Life*, January, 1974, pp. 26–37.

16 Karen Horney, M.D., *Neurosis and Human Growth* (New York and London: W.W. Norton & Co., 1950).

17 Theodore Isaac Rubin, M.D., *The Angry Book* (New York: Collier Books, 1969).

18 Erich Fromm, quoted in *The Heart Has Its Seasons*, ed. Wheaton Webb (Nashville, TN: Abingdon Press, 1982).

19 Some of the stories in the book are to be found in Hal Roach, *Laugh With the Children of Ireland* (Dublin, Ireland: Grainne Music Ltd.). Many others are from my own early recollections of stories in my neighborhood.

20 Saint Exupéry, pp. 93–94.